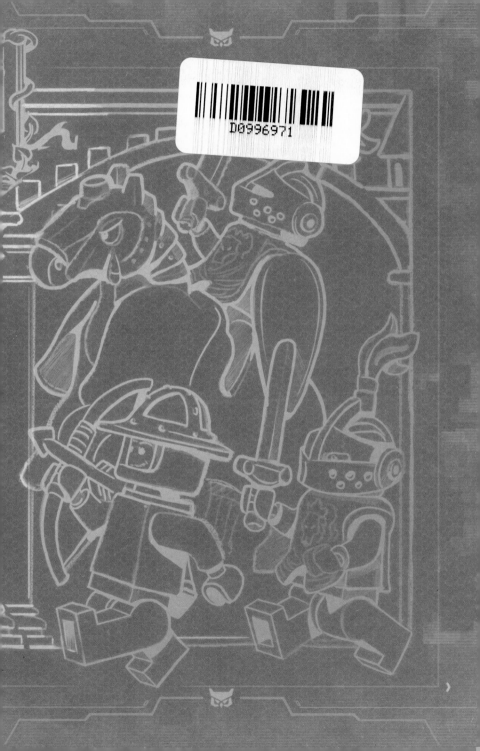

Written by: John Derevlany, Mark Hoffmeier

Creation: AMEET Studio

LEGO, the LEGO logo, the Brick and Knob configurations, the Minifigure
and NEXO KNIGHTS are trademarks of the LEGO Group.
©2016 The LEGO Group.

 Produced by AMEET Sp. z o.o.
under license from the LEGO Group.

AMEET Sp. z o.o.
Nowe Sady 6,
94-102 Łódź
ameet@ameet.pl
www.ameet.pl

www.LEGO.com

LADYBIRD BOOKS
UK | USA | Canada | Ireland | Australia | India | New Zealand | South Africa
Ladybird Books is part of the Penguin Random House group of companies
whose addresses can be found at global.penguinrandomhouse.com.
Distributed by Penguin Books Ltd, 80 Strand, London, WC2R 0RL, UK
Penguin Australia Pty Ltd: 707 Collins Street, Melbourne, VIC 3008
Penguin New Zealand Pty Ltd, 67 Apollo Drive, Rosedale, Auckland 0632
Please keep the Penguin Books Ltd address for future reference.
First published 2016
Copyright © The LEGO Group, 2016

ISBN 978-0-241-27256-5
Printed in Poland – 001

THE KNIGHT'S CODE
SQUIRE'S HANDBOOK

CONTENTS

WELCOME TO THE NEW EDITION OF THE KNIGHT'S CODE

BY THE PRINCIPAL OF THE KNIGHTS' ACADEMY,
SIR SWORDMORE BRICKLAND

The first edition of this noble book was written 500 years ago. During this time, it has helped inspire and train generations of our kingdom's greatest knights and heroes. An exact copy of the original Knight's Code text is printed in this book. Many at the Knights' Academy were reluctant to add anything to it, believing it had served us well for centuries. Why mess with perfection? But although the original Code, written by our ancestors, still remains at the core of our teaching, the world has changed dramatically over the past half a millennium, so we felt it was important to add further notes as a guide for the future Knights of the realm.

Foremost among these recent changes has been the advancement in magic and technology that has affected our land. This new edition has an additional section starting on page 57 that will fully explain the technical, conceptual and practical realities today's knights face.

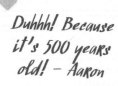

Inspire? More like put to sleep – Lance

Duhhh! Because it's 500 years old! – Aaron

Will this be on the test? Oh, wait... I've already graduated!

The Dark Ages called. They want their textbook back – Lance

CUT THAT OUT, LANCE! WE NEED TO HONOUR THE BRAVE KNIGHTS WHO WENT BEFORE US AND LAID THE FOUNDATION FOR EVERYTHING WE DO. STOP DEFACING THIS BOOK WITH YOUR DIGI-NOTES. RESPECT – CLAY

Uh . . . Clay . . . you do realize you're sticking notes in here too – Macy

Oops! She got ya there, Clay! – Aaron

BUT MINE ARE WORDS OF WISDOM . . . THAT JUST HAPPEN TO BE HANDWRITTEN. SO DON'T TREAT THESE PAGES AS SOMEWHERE YOU CAN STICK IN DOODLES OR SHOPPING LISTS.

Ooh! That reminds me: 24 eggs, 10 sticks of butter, 4 kilograms ~~of sugar~~

– Axl

STOP THAT, AXL! I SAID IT'S NOT SOMEWHERE TO STICK YOUR SHOPPING LISTS. JUST TURN THE PAGE AND READ THE REAL INTRODUCTION.

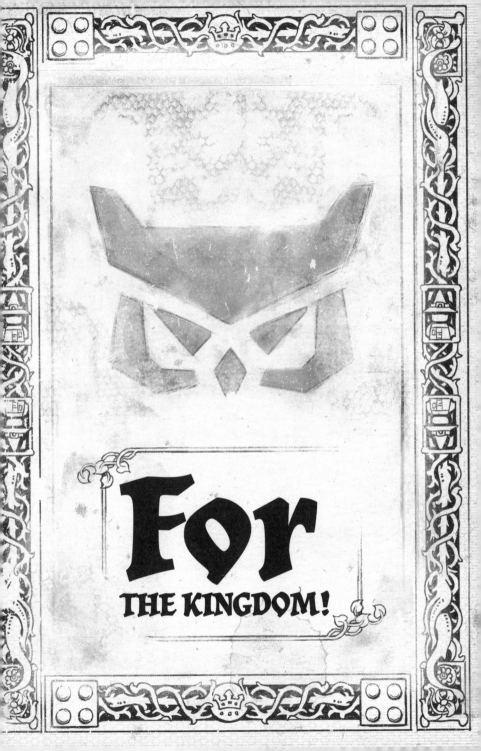

For
THE KINGDOM!

Check out that portrait of Merlok!

What . . . was he like 10 years old back then? :/

MERLOK IS MORE THAN 500 YEARS OLD. AND THIS PART OF THE BOOK WAS ONLY WRITTEN 480 YEARS AGO. SO, NO, . . . HE IS NOT TEN.

INTRODUCTION TO THE KNIGHTS' ACADEMY

by Merlok

Welcome ye aspiring knights, to the Knights' Academy – Knighton's training ground for protectors of the realm. In this academy, you will learn many important subjects including <u>history, combat, leadership skills and noble conduct</u>. But the most important thing you will learn is <u>the Knight's Code</u>.

This Code will govern your behaviour and the day-to-day choices you make. It will see you through good times and those less certain. Refer to it often.

I am the academy's resident wizard. I recently replaced the legendary <u>Gornzibarf</u> the Great who held this position for nearly a thousand years and led the school through centuries of turmoil and triumph.

Let us embark on a magical and profound journey, where you shall learn how to be future protectors, leaders and heroes, and how to be true Knights of the kingdom of Knighton.

Now get to class, students. The wonders of the kingdom await you.

What - no cooking classes?

LISTEN UP - THIS IS WHAT IT'S ALL ABOUT.

I ate too much chilli last night and I almost GornziBARFED! Ha, ha, ha!

Yeah, if he was so great, why didn't he get himself a better name?

The Knight's Code

A Knight is sworn to defend the weak, oppose the cruel and protect their kingdom.

No cause is greater than ensuring the safety of that which a Knight is sworn to protect. A Knight must be brave, stand strong, face all dangers and never give up.

All sworn duties under this Code shall be executed in a manner consistent with the Ancient Accords of Virtue and Chivalry, including its most profound pillars of Honour, Respect, Loyalty, Courage, Compassion, Diligence and Justice.

No selfish needs nor enterprise shall stop a Knight from fulfilling sworn duties under this Code. One's life is the Code; the Code is one's life.

Sworn duties under this Code shall never be executed in pursuit of personal glory, but in pursuit of excellence and the glory of the greater good.

The duties of this Code under which a Knight is sworn are of a most hallowed and noble nature and shall not be broken by any man, myth or magic. The Knight's Code is sacred and shall be treated as such.

Once sworn to the Code, a Knight cannot be unsworn.

A Knight must carry themselves with dignity and always be guided by the Code to be the best they can be.

THE HISTORY OF THE KNIGHT'S CODE

by <u>Thunderblood</u> Brickland –
Principal of the Knights' Academy

The Code of the Knighthood of Knighton (aka 'the Knight's Code') was inscribed more than a thousand years ago on a sun-dried dragon skin by the Order of the Eight – the first and most famous protectors of the land now known as Knighton. A copy of that original skin can be seen on the previous pages.

Just prior to the creation of the Code, the realm was a lawless <u>wasteland ravaged by dragons, monsters and evil creatures of all kinds</u>.

A local farmer named <u>Augustin Halbert</u> gathered seven of the bravest, strongest and most loyal citizens he could find to fight back against the evil that ruled the world around him.

13

It was a long and valiant struggle, but eventually <u>the eight</u> self-taught warriors won against their much more powerful opponents. They believed that their success was not just based on their superior intelligence and battle skills, but on something more intangible: a type of honour, loyalty and bravery that bound them together. They wanted to explain this unspoken 'code' to all the protectors of the realm who would follow in their stead.

Following their final victory over the <u>Brownwater</u> Brood of the Badlands, Halbert asked each warrior to come up with one statement or command that most effectively expressed their best behaviour and conduct. These eight statements – one from each knight – became the Code of the Knighthood of Knighton, also known as the Knight's Code.

AND I THANK THOSE EIGHT EVERY DAY FOR WHAT THEY DID!

Hee-hee! He said, 'Brownwater'. :))

Would-be knights have studied the Code and followed it for centuries. Even today, it is one of the most important documents studied and learned at this academy.

Most of the Order of the Eight went on to become the Founders of Knighton. Augustin Halbert became Knighton's first king (his family still sits on the throne). Valiant warrior Reginald Brickland started the institution that became the Knights' Academy. And Therence 'FeatherSword' Richmond – a bird catcher who became an effective warrior – founded the town of Auremville. His family became one of the wealthiest in the kingdom.

By the way, I still don't know it.

Yes, we know. :P

They called your ancestor FeatherSword?

Yeah! Feathers were really tough in the old days.

What, did he tickle his opponents to death?

I like catching birds! Especially . . . fried chickens!

WILL YOU GUYS PLEASE TAKE THIS SERIOUSLY?

WELCOME TO THE KNIGHTS' ACADEMY

N ow that you students have studied, memorized and dedicated your life to the Knight's Code, it is time for you to become better acquainted with the dawn-to-dusk training, studying, and strong commitment to the pursuit of greatness that will be your next four years here at <u>the Knights' Academy</u>. As a direct descendant of the Great Reginald Brickland, one of the founders and creators of the Knight's Code and this Knights' Academy, I, <u>Thunderblood Brickland</u> have dedicated my life to

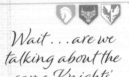

Wait . . . are we talking about the same Knights' Academy that I went to? :-/

Nah, this part of the book was written, like, 500 years ago. Ignore it.

WHAT? THIS IS ESSENTIAL READING. PAY ATTENTION! :X

No way! Is that his real name? :-0

turning you meek and helpless <u>little children</u> into great knights and protectors of the realm. You may <u>struggle and suffer</u> at times. You may even ask yourself, '<u>Am I strong enough . . . am I smart enough . . . am I noble enough to be a True Knight</u>?' But always remember this: bricks together are unbreakable.

You will learn much in your time here at the academy. Most importantly, you will learn that a castle is only as strong as its weakest brick. And you shall, as knights of Knighton, become <u>the strongest, smartest and most noble bricks</u> the realm has ever known. This shall be your mission, your duty and your life's work. In a few short years, you will become Knights of Knighton. Or, as I like to say, 'the bricks that guard our land'.

Good luck, students!
Your kingdom awaits its Protectors.

Thunderblood Brickland

Knights' Academy Principal

For the record, I was NEVER little. ;))

I'm suffering now just reading this. :(

YES, YES AND YES! =D

Uh . . . Are we building castles here or learning how to become knights? I'm confused.

I think he just likes to talk about bricks because his name is BRICKland. ;)

ACADEMY CLASS SCHEDULE

All students at the Knights' Academy are expected to complete their studies and training in <u>four years</u> of learning, both inside the classroom and out on the training ground. Each year focuses on a different aspect of your knight's training. Here is what you can expect in your extremely <u>demanding and unforgiving time</u> at the Knights' Academy.

BEST. FOUR. YEARS. EVER.

Oh, please . . . It wasn't that bad.

Novice? More like 'total newbie'! :P

YEAR ONE - <u>NOVICE</u>

Introduction to the Knight's Code: Basics of Knighthood

Chivalry and Ethics 101

Is it bad if you cheat on your ethics test? ;)

Combat Skills – Level 1: Swords and Axes

Beginner's Metallurgy and Protective Armour

Introduction to Equestrian Skills and Horsemanship

If it looks like a horse and hovers – I am ON it!

Uh, this part of the book is so old – these were actual real horses . . . with legs.

Ewww! Gross!

Castle Economics (voluntary)

Creative Tapestry-making (voluntary)

YEAR TWO – APPRENTICE

The History of Knighton

What . . . no digi-arrows? Dude, this is so medieval!

Combat Skills – Level 2: Bowmanship and Range Weapons

Chivalry Honours

Advanced Metallurgy and Protective Armour

Advanced Horsemanship and Jousting

Jousting Bieber was around back then?

Er, you're kidding, right? :-/

Technology (from alchemy to magic)

Huh? That's the 'technology' class? :-?

Physical Education

Horse Cart Mechanics (voluntary)

What's a 'horse cart'?

Woodwork and Forest Monsters (voluntary)

YEAR THREE – WEAPON BEARER

Geography of Knighton

Combat Skills – Level 3: Battlefield and Siege Tactics

I THINK WE HAVE ALL ALREADY BEEN INTRODUCED TO THEM. B-)

Introduction to Monsters (lab, plus fieldwork)

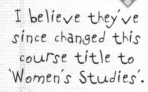

I believe they've since changed this course title to 'Women's Studies'.

Damsel in Distress 101

Foreign Language – choose from: Latin, French or Monster Growl

I'm a master in Monster Growl: eRRRR, aghRRR, bllll ;P

First Aid 101 – from dried toads to leeches

O.K, seriously? Is that the best 'medicine' they had? :-O

Physical Education

Ballroom Dancing (voluntary)

THIS IS VOLUNTARY? THAT'S UP FOR DEBATE. HA, HA, HA!

Wait... did Clay just make a joke? ;))

Diplomacy /Debate (voluntary)

YEAR FOUR – SQUIRE

Combat Skills – Level 4: Prolonged Military Campaigns and Battles

Advanced Monsters (students must have already taken: Combat 3, First Aid 101)

History of the Royal Families of Knighton

Field Study (students must go on a quest)

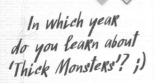

In which year do you learn about 'Thick Monsters'? ;)

Every year! Ha, ha, ha! :P

Believe it or not, I only got a 'B' in this. :-/

Posing Heroically

Ha! I could've taught this class!

Modern Ballistics and Machines (Is the catapult the weapon of the future?)

No,

Physical Education

Legend Building (voluntary)

My legend was already built. B-)

Pottery and Ceramics (voluntary)

Ooh! My favourite! :))

GRADUATION – SHIELD BEARER

Upon completion of all the required <u>courses</u> and one voluntary course in each year of enrolment, students will receive the Knights' Academy Degree of Knighthood. Graduates will also be awarded their Knight's Shield and become official Protectors of the Realm.

Sweet shields! :))

Yeah, but can they get a digi-download? The answer is no.

THEY DIDN'T NEED DOWNLOADS OF NEXO POWERS BACK THEN. BUT WE DEFINITELY NEED THEM NOW. :)

Did I ever tell you how much I liked my Pottery and Ceramics class? I drew a picture of one of the coffee mugs I made. :))

CODE OF CONDUCT

Enrolment in the Knights' Academy is considered one of the highest <u>privileges</u> granted to the youth of Knighton. You have been chosen to be future Protectors of the Realm and saviours of all that is worth saving. You are the next generation of the Knights of Knighton. As such, you will be expected to conduct yourselves in accordance with the principles set forth below.

I just got a coupon for 'One free ice cream' from Sir Scoopsalot's shop. Now that's a privilege.

You will always <u>follow the Knight's Code</u> and apply it to all decisions and actions while at the academy.

All right already! We get it – follow the Code!

You will always <u>seek justice, fairness and safety</u> for the king and the kingdom of Knighton.

Done! :>

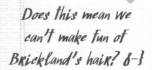

Does this mean we can't make fun of Brickland's hair? 8-}

You will show <u>respect</u> to all the teachers and administrators of the Knights' Academy.

You shall also treat your fellow students with respect and fairness. All are equal at the Knights' Academy.

Ah, that's easy. I just wipe my armour with my underpants! :))

That is so totally not appropriate. :/

It's not? Oh … I'd better let Lance know then. He paid me to clean his armour too.

What?
AHHHH!

Armour shall be <u>polished regularly</u> using appropriate cleaning and shining agents.

Spending time with monsters or evildoers of any kind is <u>strictly forbidden</u>.

Works for me! B-)

Recreational belching, gulping, snorting and/or breaking wind is <u>strictly prohibited</u>. As per the Fox Rule, no exceptions are allowed.

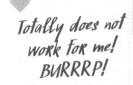

Totally does not work for me! BURRRP!

All meals shall be consumed in the dining hall during dining hours, unless one can prove a need for <u>additional nutrition</u>.

Where do I get a doctor's note for this? :-/

Breaking any part of this code shall result in a student receiving a black mark on his/her permanent record.

Keep this book and its contents <u>secret</u>. Share its contents with no one.

But how are we supposed to keep this secret? /:)

Like this: 'Hey, if you're reading this right now and you're not a knight, raise your hand.' Hmm . . . I don't see anyone raising their hand. So we're all good. B-)

*No, this is nuts!
The old days were
soooo lame.*

COURSE MATERIALS REQUIRED

Attendance at the Knights' Academy requires all students to come to class prepared with one or more of the following materials:

Six rolls of parchment or properly cured animal skin to be used for taking notes

*What if the feather
quill is still
attached to the bird?
Will that be OK?*

Two sharpened quills made of bird feathers (duck or goose preferred)

One full bottle of ink (made of charcoal or iron residue)

Thirty pieces of coal for the classroom furnace

Seriously? No central heating?

Three separate servings of gruel (one lunch portion, two snack-sized)

I see the words 'lunch' and 'snack', but what's this 'gruel' stuff? :-/

One complete set of chain mail and armour (for combat classes only)

It'd be pretty funny to wear your armour to art class.

Or to ballroom dancing. <-P

BORKRRING! (-)

One practice sword (wooden)

NOW WE'RE TALKING! :))

One broadsword (iron)

You don't get your real shield until you graduate . . . or in my case, until your father, the king, says it's OK.

One apprentice shield

And that dummy's name is Clay! Ha! Just kidding, Clay.

One combat practice dummy

Additional combat tools and weapons may be needed in particular classes

I BRING EVERYTHING WITH ME, JUST IN CASE. :)

Yes . . . we know . . .

In addition, proper classroom attire is required at all times, including <u>woollen trousers, horsehair cloak, animal skin shirt and tunic</u>. The student is responsible for buying all class materials from the appropriate merchants, blacksmiths and/or alchemists. Failing to bring any of the above items to class will result in disciplinary action. <u>No excuses will be accepted</u>.

Huh? No T-shirts? :-/

Oh, c'mon . . . how about this excuse: 'My combat dummy was so dumb he got lost on the way to class!'

'The dog ate my parchment!'

'SORRY I'm not dressed properly but my "tunic" was "out of tune"!' Ha, ha, ha, ha! :P

GUYS, THEY WERE SERIOUS BACK THEN . . . TURN THE PAGE!

DISCIPLINARY ACTIONS

A true Knight *always* does the right thing without fail and without hesitation. Students who are *studying* to be knights, however, sometimes need to be reminded of their proper duties and responsibilities under the rules of the Knights' Academy. Failure to follow any of the rules shall result in disciplinary action, ranging from a minor tickling to a long stay in the academy's dungeon. In addition, breaking the rules will result in one black mark being added to a student's permanent record. The accumulation of three black marks shall result in a scroll from the principal being sent home to a student's guardian by carrier pigeon or horse messenger.

WHAT?
Are they serious?

They were pretty strict back then. Things were a lot more relaxed by the time we got there.

What? No email? :-O

Oh, come on! Dude, if they still did that when we were there, they would've renamed the dungeon 'Aaron's Bedroom'.

WELL, AT LEAST YOU GET THREE MEALS.

Yum . . . Salted mud . . . 8->

Five or more black marks on a student's permanent record shall result in the student being assigned detention in the <u>academy's dungeon</u> for a minimum of fifteen days. Repeated rule-breaking will result in detention, suspension and/or ninety days chained up in the academy's dungeon with only <u>salted mud to eat for breakfast, lunch and dinner</u>.

Bad behaviour liable to give you a black mark include:

- **Failure to complete all schoolwork or homework**

- **Failure to bring sufficient course materials to class or fieldwork**

- **Failure to respect the academy staff**

- **Failure to memorize and fulfil the Knight's Code**

Yep, I've probably done all of that and more.

Check, check, check and check! :-)

In addition, attendance is compulsory for all classes and after-school functions. There are only three acceptable excuses for failing to attend any of the academy's scheduled events. These include . . .

You can't get out of bed due to a severe case of the plague

Does a really bad stomach ache count as the plague?

You have been eaten by a dragon

I tried using this excuse once. Trust me, it doesn't work.

You have an excuse from the king

Of course, I would NEVER ask my father to write me an excuse. Tee-hee-hee!

A STUDENT'S DAILY SCHEDULE

_What?
No digitally
monitored goose-
feather mattress?
This isn't school!
It's torture!_

4 a.m.
Wake up, get out of a bed made of <u>solid wood</u> and straw.

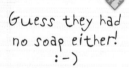

_I bet they spent
all day scratching
their bottoms!_

4 a.m. – 4:30 a.m.
Remove bed splinters from back and <u>clean extra straw out of underwear</u>.

4:30 a.m. – 5 a.m.
<u>Retrieve water from well for shower</u>.

GUESS THEY HAD NO
INDOOR PLUMBING. :-/

5 a.m. – 6 a.m.
Start fire and heat water for shower.

6 a.m. – 6:05 a.m.
Take shower; wash skin with <u>soft rocks and butter fat</u>.

_Guess they had
no soap either!
:-)_

6:05 a.m. – 7 a.m.
Avoid insects attracted by smell of butter fat on your skin.

7 a.m. – 8 a.m.
Milk cows, collect eggs, pick bugs out of <u>porridge</u>.

8 a.m. – 8:30 a.m.
Eat breakfast.

8:30 a.m. – 11 a.m.
Castle chores – cleaning and scrubbing the castle and removing the principal's scabs and ingrown toenails.

11 a.m. – 1:30 p.m.
Hunt for lunch.

1:30 a.m. – 2 p.m.
Start fire for lunch.

2 p.m. – 2:30 p.m.
Cook and eat lunch caught that morning.

2:30 p.m. – 3 p.m.
Attend <u>classes</u> in knight-related subjects.

I actually know a good recipe for porridge bugs. :P

I believe I speak for all of us when I say: Ewwwwww!

Dudes, are there only thirty minutes of classes a day?

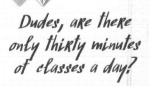

YES, AS A MATTER OF FACT, JUST SURVIVING IN THOSE DAYS WAS SO CHALLENGING, THERE WASN'T MUCH TIME FOR CLASSES.

3 p.m. – 3:30 p.m.
Prepare traps and gear for afternoon hunting expedition.

3:30 p.m. – 5 p.m.
Hunt for dinner.

5 p.m.– 6 p.m.
Prepare dinner with other knights.

6 p.m. – 7 p.m.
<u>Deal with stomach ache</u>.

THAT'S FROM EATING IMPROPERLY PREPARED AND STORED FOOD PRODUCTS.

7 p.m. – 8 p.m.
Have it treated by in-house doctor, who can prescribe <u>leeches</u> and bloodletting for stomach ache.

I actually know a good recipe for leeches too! :))

8 p.m. – 8:05 p.m.
<u>Homework</u>.

Five minutes of homework? Old Times Rule!

8:05 p.m. – 9 p.m.
Finish castle chores, including scrubbing of principal's bedpan.

9 p.m. – 10 p.m.
Extra credit courses – for those students
hoping to graduate the academy
on time.

10 p.m. – 10:30 p.m.
Gather <u>more straw for bed</u>.

10:30 p.m. – 4 a.m.
Sleep if you have completed all your
chores and/or survived.

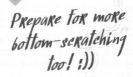

PRepaRe foR moRe
bottom-scRatching
too! :))

I have to say
I'm glad we
didn't go to the
academy back
then. :-|

Me too!

Not me! BaRely
any classes,
just hunting and
sleeping! Woo-hoo!
BRing on the butter
fat showers!

A GUIDE TO MODERN WEAPONS

As a student at the Knights' Academy, you will have access to the best weapons available in the kingdom today. We have had a team of blacksmiths and alchemists working around the sundial to build you some of <u>the finest weapons in the realm</u>. Prepare to be wowed, young apprentice. This is the future of battle.

FOR REAL? A CHILD KNOWS HOW TO MAKE THOSE. :D

THE SWORD

One of a knight's main tools of combat is the sword, which can be used both to strike an opponent and to deflect an opponent's attack.

Below you will find a diagram pinpointing the many important parts of the sword and how our experts here at the Knights' Academy have improved upon them.

THE BLADE – for many years, this cutting and thrusting part of the sword was made of copper, iron, or even very sharp rocks. But our weapon-smiths have begun building swords with a revolutionary new material called '<u>steel</u>'. It is stronger, lighter and more durable.

They just figured out what a steel blade is? Ughhhh . . .

THE CROSS GUARD –

this sits between the end of the blade and the beginning of the grip; used to protect a knight's hand in battle.

IF ONLY IT COULD DOWNLOAD NEXO POWERS LIKE MY CLAYMORE SWORD.

THE GRIP – new advancements in fabric-making have allowed us to cover the handle of the sword with a protective material. Until recently, the grip was sharp and metal like the blade, and this had a <u>bad impact on the user's hand and fingers</u> . . . if one had any left.

Yikes! How long did it take them to work that out?

I'm counting the years – on my fingers, which I still have!

ARMOUR

Some of our main achievements in the world of combat technology have been to do with reducing the weight of the armour our knights wear. We have succeeded in lowering its bulk from nearly twenty stone to just over fifteen stone. Yes, the armour still weighs more than the average warrior who wears it, but at least future knights will actually be able to move during battle.

HELMET – previous efforts to protect one's head with coconut shells have been replaced by the metal helmet. Coming in at a weight of only five stone, it will compress the average user's neck like an accordion within two hours of continuous wear. But at least the warrior's <u>face will be safe</u>.

Phew! That's a relief. I like my face.

Yum . . . coconuts 8->

BREASTPLATE – this area has been reinforced with both steel and concrete to protect the chest.

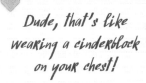

Dude, that's like wearing a cinderblock on your chest!

GAUNTLETS – these actually do nothing, but our fashion-forward armour designer insisted that they tie the whole outfit together.

ARMOURED LEGGINGS – leggings are still heavy and unwieldy. However, advancements now allow knights to bend their knees almost five degrees. It's not quite enough to allow a knight to walk properly, but it comes in handy if you need to step over a <u>small rock</u>.

Look out, small rocks! We're coming for you!

Are they serious? A knight's crest represents their family and their kingdom! :-/

Sorry, Macy, I have to agree — if the shield can't fly, it's totally useless.

With my shield I can actually serve those snacks and microwave them at the same time! :P

A KNIGHT'S CREST AND SHIELD ARE ALMOST AS IMPORTANT AS THE CODE AND FOLLOWING ITS RULES. THEY ARE ONE'S PRIDE, PROTECTION AND SIGN OF UNITY.

THE SHIELD

This is a <u>mostly useless piece of armour</u>, and will never play any significant role in a knight's duty. The chief purpose of the shield is to hide any flaws and rust spots in the body armour. It is extremely demoralizing to walk onto the battlefield with an unsightly scuff or tarnish on one's breastplate. The most you can ever hope to do with your shield is hang it on a wall, or serve your friends dinner snacks on it.

FRONT OF SHIELD – nothing to see here. Except maybe some crests or other doodles used to distract an opponent.

BACK OF SHIELD – even less to see here.
<u>This is where you hold it</u>.

. . . and this is
how you stand
when you're
flying. ;)

THE LIMB – this is a highly bendy piece of material that used to be made of goat horn. But the academy's weapon-smiths now use a type of treated <u>birchwood or elm</u>.

THE STRING – earlier versions of the string were made of celery fibres and beeswax. We have since improved our string by reinforcing the celery fibres with <u>toad spit</u>.

Bet the goats are really happy about that :)

No way, dudes! If I find any toad spit on my bow, I'm switching to a sword!

THE BOW AND ARROW

Weapons which fire arrows are quite a new achievement in the world of <u>modern combat</u>. Again, our weapon-smiths have been working hard to improve this newfangled device.

THE ARROW – now nearly ninety per cent of our arrows are almost straight. The other ten per cent, well . . . <u>three students last year</u> ended up shooting themselves in the rear with their own arrows.

THE ARROWHEAD – large rocks have been replaced with sleek, polished blades. We've attached these blades to the shafts with that same toad spit we used on the strings, but they don't stay on very well. This is very much a work in progress.

Modern? /:)

Only three? They must have been really good shots. :P

I think I'd rather be a damsel in distress than an archer in those days!

There are many more weapons available to the aspiring knight. But realistically, <u>they're all useless</u>.

Hey, I love my axe! :-*

And my lance! :))

And my mace . . . well, at least the modern version of it. :P

Or . . . you just skipped ahead to the end! That's what I did.

Clay took this part quite literally – he always has this book pretty much glued to his hand. :D

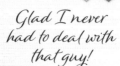

Glad I never had to deal with that guy!

Yeah, but we still had to deal with the other Brickland.

Congratulations, aspiring Knights of the realm! By making it to the final page of this Knight's Code handbook, you have most likely navigated your first <u>few years of training at the Knights' Academy</u>. By getting this far, you stand a very good chance of living to the ripe old age of fifteen, and even possibly becoming a valuable knight.

All of us at the Knights' Academy and in the kingdom of Knighton are extremely proud of you and wish you much success in your service ahead. <u>Please keep this book close to hand</u> so you can use it to remind yourself of your important duties as a knight. We will be updating this volume often so it always stays current with all knightly trends.

For the academy, for the king, and for the Knight's Code . . .

Thunderblood Brickland

THE KNIGHT'S CODE: UPDATE

WRITTEN AND ADDED BY PRINCIPAL BRICKLAND

Aha, here's our Brickland!

And our times!

THE KNIGHTS' ACADEMY CAMPUS

THE KNIGHTS' ACADEMY MOTTO:
'UT AD ARMA, ATQUE AD PROTEGENDUM!'
('Learning to Shield and to Protect!')

The Knights' Academy is located in the heart of the capital city of Knightonia, and has been training Knights of the realm for over 400 years. Now, it trains knights who come here to hone their skills, their knowledge and their chivalry.

THE MAIN BUILDING
Houses the main foyer, cafeteria, auditorium and most classrooms.

THE GRAND ENTRANCE
Dedicated years ago to King Pike VII.

THE CAFETERIA
Where delicious food is served.

You know what I liked best about the campus? The cafeteria. :)

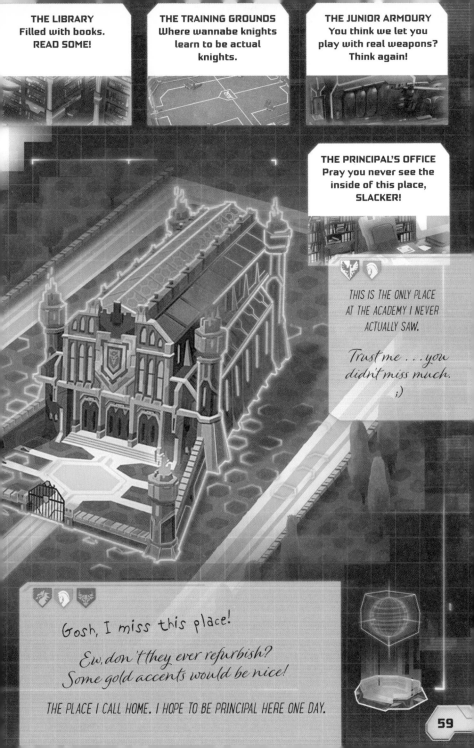

THE LIBRARY
Filled with books.
READ SOME!

THE TRAINING GROUNDS
Where wannabe knights
learn to be actual
knights.

THE JUNIOR ARMOURY
You think we let you
play with real weapons?
Think again!

THE PRINCIPAL'S OFFICE
Pray you never see the
inside of this place,
SLACKER!

THIS IS THE ONLY PLACE
AT THE ACADEMY I NEVER
ACTUALLY SAW.

Trust me . . . you
didn't miss much.
;)

Gosh, I miss this place!

Ew, don't they ever refurbish?
Some gold accents would be nice!

THE PLACE I CALL HOME. I HOPE TO BE PRINCIPAL HERE ONE DAY.

59

THE LIBRARY

> *I hate the library.*
> *So much reading.*
> *I paid someone*
> *to read for me.*
>
> *This was the best*
> *place to catch*
> *some ZZZZs.*

The <u>Library</u> is filled with books. Books that will help you learn things and be able to graduate from this glorious institution. The best thing you can do while you're here is stick your nose in a library book and NEVER DO ANYTHING ELSE!

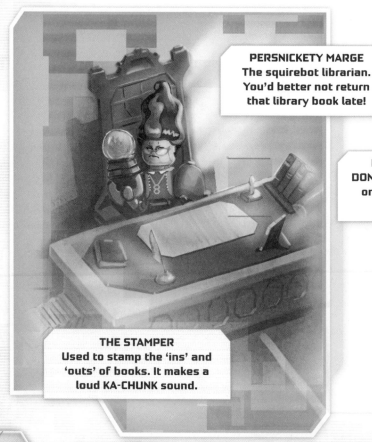

PERSNICKETY MARGE
The squirebot librarian. You'd better not return that library book late!

MARGE'S DESK
DON'T touch anythi
on it! (If you value
your health!)

THE STAMPER
Used to stamp the 'ins' and 'outs' of books. It makes a loud KA-CHUNK sound.

I SPENT MOST OF MY SPARE TIME HERE. OK – I SPENT <u>ALL</u> OF MY SPARE TIME HERE.

TRAINING GROUND

A strong body is as important as a strong mind, and knights are made on the training grounds. This is where you practise your teamwork, your moves and become a physically imposing knight of the realm.

I named my first training lance, Lance. He was my biggest fan.

THE ARMAMENTS RACK
Pick your best weapon and learn how to use it.

THE SIDELINES
Where you get timed to see just how quickly you can beat the other team.

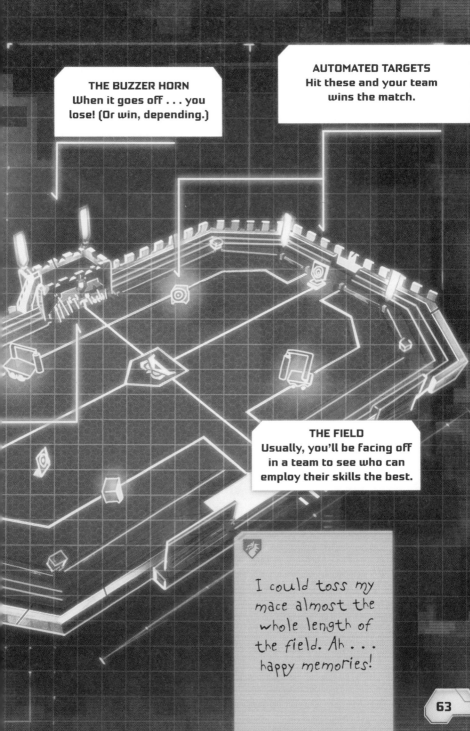

I once shot an apple off the top of some kid's head in this very place, I'm so cool.

CAFETERIA

The cafeteria is <u>where every knight-in-training eats</u> – in an orderly manner – and doesn't spend too much time fooling around. If you want to really be tough, you can order a rock sandwich for lunch. Not good for your teeth, but it makes you look cool.

THE KITCHEN
Famous chef Gobbleton Rambley created the menu. So if you don't like it, he'll yell at you until you do.

My happiest moments at the Knights' Academy happened here.

THE SERVING LINE
C'mon, keep moving! Everybody needs to eat before lunchtime is over! Stop lollygagging!

SWEETS
There are NO SWEETS
HERE! Stop looking
for sweets!

THE MILK MACHINE
It dispenses MILK! What did
you think came out of it?

*ALWAYS DRINK LOTS OF
MILK. IT'S HOW I GOT SO
BIG AND STRONG.*

TABLES
The tables in the dining
hall were built by the
royal carpenter himself,
Sir Woody Carverer. They're
all perfectly flat.

THE DISHWASHER
Where students who
haven't done their
homework go.

CLASSROOMS

The King Pike IX Learning Centre houses most of the Knights' Academy classroom space. It was King Pike IX who first gave some gold to build this structure, replacing the academy's original classroom, which consisted of muck-filled yurts with dirt floors. (Personally, I think that the students have been too soft ever since.)

THE MERLOK MAGIC LABS
A series of labs where magical experiments and learning can happen in <u>relative safety.</u>

Summon
a giant
chimera
always a g
opportuni
to practi
lab safet
procedure

THE SHARPENING ROOM
Learn to be sharper.

THE MATHS ROOM
Where your brain goes to experience overheating.

THE JOKES KNIGHTLY LANGUAGE LAB
Sponsored by comedian Jokes Knightly when he was still rich and famous, this is <u>where you can learn to converse with dragons or dwarves</u>.

THE CHAIN MAIL ROOM
How to handle your chain mail. There's a test . . . be ready.

THE CLASSROOM OF CLASSROOMS
Where you learn how to learn. Oh, and you have to do a final project about doing final projects.

THE BRICKNEY SPEARS SPEAR-LEARNING ANNEX
In this classroom – sponsored by the famous Knighton pop star – you'll learn everything you ever wanted to know about a spear . . . and more!

THE ART ROOM
Paint your coat of arms – burnt umber is a great base colour.

WEAPON MAINTENANCE

The following is a list of Weapon Maintenance Classes that you must take in order to graduate from the Knights' Academy:

LEVEL ONE

- Introduction to Weapon Cleaning: a clean weapon is a happy weapon.
- Introduction to Weapon Maintenance: maintain it or it will fall apart.
- Polishing Skills for the New Student: <u>make it shine, people</u>.
- Sheathing: your weapon should be warm and cosy.

LEVEL TWO

- Advanced Weapon Cleaning: polishing with a toothbrush.
- Advanced Weapon Maintenance: take it apart and put it back together while blindfolded.
- Oils, Waxes, Polishes and Sealers: know them by smell.
- Introduction to Sharpening: life's a grind, sometimes.

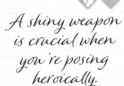

A shiny weapon is crucial when you're posing heroically.

Hey Lance, do you use the same wax for polishing your lance as you do for your hair?

I'll have to check with Dennis.

LEVEL THREE

- Cleaning Master Class: blind others with your shiny sword.
- Maintenance Master Class: <u>take apart a mace and turn it into a sword</u>.
- Advanced Sharpening: make your sword sharp enough to cut rocks in half.
- Arrows for Fun and Profit: make them, trade them, shoot 'em at targets!

No way! My mace is aMACYing!

OPEN LEVEL CLASSES

- Pikes and Poleaxes: keep the bad guys at a distance.
- Shields and Helmets: stay safe on the battlefield.
- <u>Naming Your Weapons</u>: treat them like your best friends!
- Magic Weapons: they give you such an edge.

I call mine 'My Sweet Candy'!

I named my lances after the most gallant servants of the Richmond family.

YOU MEAN YOUR NANNIES, RIGHT?

POETRY AND SERENADING

Learning to be a well-rounded young knight involves more skills than shining your armour and cleaving things in half. You also need to be chivalrous in your use of words. A top knight should be good at poetry and serenading. Here are some examples. (Written by myself, yours truly, of course.)

EXAMPLES OF FINE POETRY:

'Roses are red,
violets are blue,
that puny shield
will not protect you.'

'Arrows, arrows everywhere,
And all the monsters cried.
Arrows, arrows everywhere . . .
The enemy was *fried*.'

'In Knightonia did King Halbert
A Knights' Academy decree:
To protect his realm and lands,
From merciless monster bands,
From the mountains to the sea.'

'Roses are red,
violets are blue,
I always eat muffins
and leave none for you!'

All of the knights
went out to see a movie
Except for Clay –
no one told him
it was today!

TIPS FOR SERENADING:

- Learn to play a lute, because if you play a horn you can't sing and play at the same time.
- Warm up your voice before serenading. I do this by randomly yelling at things.
- Pick songs that mention sunsets, love and flowers, not those that mention monsters, pointy pikes, or magical melty things.
- Always carry flowers without thorns when serenading.
- Make sure you brush your teeth and wax your nose hair before serenading.
- Singing the Knights' Academy School Song is good training for serenading.
- You can often disarm an enemy by <u>suddenly serenading them</u>.

All of the knights were out on a quest. Except for Aaron – he was at home, sleeping like a baron!

ALL OF THE KNIGHTS WERE BATTLING MONSTERS EXCEPT FOR MACY – SHE WAS AT HOME PLAYING WITH A DOLL NAMED TRACY!

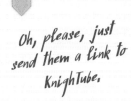

Oh, please, just send them a link to KnighTube.

VEHICLES AND HOW TO DRIVE THEM

An important part of being a modern knight is knowing how to properly handle vehicles of all kinds. Here are some useful tips for driving these vehicles. (Not that I've driven all of them, but I'm the principal here and therefore *always* know best about everything.)

GENERAL VEHICLE DRIVING TIPS:

- Keep your eyes on the road and off the KnightNet while you're driving! (That's an order!)
- Make sure your tyres and wheels have no arrows or crossbow bolts stuck in them.
- Wash and wax your vehicle before every battle.
- Clean all blasters and pointy bits.
- Keep all lava away from your engine.
- NEVER brake for monsters.
- TURN THAT RADIO DOWN!

Always drive this like you're the shiniest, shallowest, most ready-to-fool-around knight there is. I mean, only a Richmond looks good driving a mechanical horse that converts into a motorcycle.

ANY <u>REAL</u> KNIGHT WANTS TO RIDE IN A SWORD-SHAPED VEHICLE. JUST BE CAREFUL NOT TO HIT THE BIG RED BUTTON THAT SHOOTS THE SWORD PART INTO THE AIR LIKE A ROCKET.

Remember this tip: AATTT – Always Accelerate Through The Target! Any monster will be toast. (Or magical ether, as the case may be.)

PHYSICAL EDUCATION

If you can't do a thousand press-ups in fifteen minutes, you should flunk yourself out of the academy right now! That said, physical education is something that lets you work towards goals, and is one of the most important aspects of being a knight. Hey, if you're not in shape (like me) you can't swing that heavy sword 100 or so times at that giant monster.

SOME OF THE PHYSICAL EDUCATION CLASSES OFFERED AT THE KNIGHTS' ACADEMY:

<u>INTRODUCTION TO RUNNING</u> – Running, followed by some running, with a break for some running.

MACE MASHING 101 – Goal: mace 100 things with your mace in under ninety seconds.

ARMOURED YOGA – You may be in ten-stone armour, but you should still be able to wrap your legs around your head. DO IT!

PIKE VAULTING – Can you <u>clear that castle</u> wall? You'd better!

Oh, that's something for Jestro!

I have everything cleared up by Dennis.

Er, Lance, it is not <u>that</u> kind of clearing they are talking about . . .

THE HAMMER THROW – Queen Halbert still holds the academy's record.

ADVANCED BOW PULLING – Can you fire 100 arrows in under a minute? You can't? You're worthless and weak.

ADVANCED RUNNING – Running further, followed by running longer, with tips for running faster (such as me following you on a hover horse with a spear!).

MASTER THE AXE – First you start by chopping piles of wood. Then you move on to chopping piles of monsters.

SPEARING – Before you learn to throw a spear, you must learn to *be* a spear. Seriously, stand still while I throw you at the target.

<u>**MASTER ADVANCE RUNNING**</u> – Just run. Until I tell you to stop. Which will be in about a week from now. RUN!

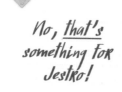

No, that's something for Jestro!

EXPLORE THE CAMPUS

Many a knight in the kingdom longs for the golden days of vigorous study at the academy. But it isn't all studying. Academy life is full of, well . . . life.

Baking Club! Where you learn to make soufflés worthy of knights. ;)

But there was never anything left to eat after you joined the club!

EXTRACURRICULAR ACTIVITIES
The great majority of these are not curricular . . . they are extracurricular. Everything from theatre (about knights) to debate clubs (debating knights) and baking club.

THE WISHING WELL
Its cornerstone was laid by King Halbert himself – he loves to toss in a coin and wish someone well.

THE ELECTRIC LUTE ROOM
A good place to cut loose on your electric lute, hyper harp, or harpsicordian.

Well, only the extreme nerds can actually master the harpsicordian.

THE SHRUB OF TRUTH
Lovely topiary donated by some studious computer-science students. It will actually attempt to answer every question put to it.

CHIVALROUS ROOM
There are many spots on campus where you can contemplate chivalrous thoughts: the gardens, the library . . . the CHIVALROUS ROOM where you can practise chivalrousness with a squirebot trained by Haute Fancypants, the King's own servant.

THE ATTIC OF STUFF
Many a student will do their voluntary clean-up duty in the attic of the academy, simply to see all the wondrous things there, including: Ned Knightly's toenail clippings (not authenticated) and Sir Griffiths' stuffed pet griffin, who he named Griff.

Shouldn't it be a damsel instead of a bot?

No damsel could bear your attempts at chivalry! :)

THE PATH OF ENLIGHTENMENT
Stepping stones in the garden that lay out some good tips for leading a knightly life. Tip Number One: pretend that everywhere except for these stepping stones is lava . . . now! Don't fall into the lava!

THE POLISH PARLOUR
Have some extra coinage? Get the squirebots in this space to do all your polishing for you.

FESTIVALS AND COMPETITIONS

The Knights' Academy trains students to be the ultimate competitors. Naturally, festivals and competitions (and festivals *about* competitions) are a vital part of academy life.

THE PRINCIPAL'S TOURNAMENT
The end-of-the-academic-year festival that lets students of every level show off their skills. Everyone wants to win 'Brickland's Brick' – the tournament's ultimate trophy.

BOWDACIOUS DAY
A chance to show what can be done with a bow or crossbow. Shoot targets, split apples on top of friends' heads, play your bow like a guitar . . . it's all part of Bowdacious Day!

That's my day!

ARMOUR DAY
Students get a chance to show off their best armour.

And that's MY day. What armour is best? The shiny stuff!

SPRING JOUST
Grab a hover horse, a lance, a quality helmet and someone to play against and get out there. Then try to knock each other off!

AUTUMN THEATRE FEST

Enjoy classic plays by Quakespear, the most famous ancient playwright in Knighton. This year saw a production of his most <u>popular play, Hammerlet</u>.

My favourite is 'Titus Brickonicus'. I could easily play in both.

THE ALUMNI TOURNAMENT

A chance for the students <u>to battle some famous alumni</u>.

You'll let Brickland win if you know what's good for you.

THE SINGING SWORD SONG COMPETITION

A chance to have your name engraved on the Singing Sword for the boomiest voice of any academy student.

THE QUEEN OF CLEAN FESTIVAL

Grab a hammer and re-shingle the roof to the Grand Hall! This festival was founded by Queen Halbert who loves to hammer.

<u>THE 'DANCE 'TIL YOU DROP' WINTER FORMAL</u>

Put on your best clothes, and you and your date must try to be the last couple dancing, to win this combination prom/competition.

THE CURRENT RECORD IS ELEVEN DAYS.

And it belongs to my mum. Again.

CHIVALRY DEBATE TOURNAMENT

Placing your cloak over a puddle or using your helmet to boil soup for hungry orphans – which is more chivalrous? Argue it out at the tournament!

CLUBS AND GROUPS

What sort of clubs and groups might there be at the Knights' Academy? Glad you asked! There are many organizations for you to join:

Poleaxes are good for scratching your back with! :)

KNIGHT CLUB
Earn your merit badges for knightly activities such as: chain mail repair, wound lancing, digital fire building and finding <u>other uses for a poleaxe</u>.

THE KINGSMEN

I was there!

The official academy glee club that sings updated arrangements of old classics like 'Cut-out that Dragon's Tongue' (the mech-hop update), 'Boiled in Oil, Oil, Oil!' and 'The Sword Swingers' Theme in C-Sharp'.

CLUB CLUB
Gotta collect them all.

Collect, trade and use <u>your favourite clubs</u> with your academy peers.

SWIM CLUB
Yeah, you attended each club. Just once.

Can you actually swim in armour? You're going to find out.

ARCHERS ANONYMOUS
For the kids that just gotta shoot, shoot, shoot arrows.

SHIELDS AND SPEARS
The club for students in <u>the upper ten per cent of their class</u>.

I FELT PRETTY LONELY IN THIS CLUB.

STUDY OR GET EXPELLED
The club for students in <u>the lower ten per cent of their class</u>.

I didn't feel lonely here. It's an elite club. Deal with it.

HELMET HAIR
Grooming tips for everyone who wears armour.

SYNCHRONIZED SPEARING
Can you dance and hurl a spear at the same time? I bet you can!

DUNGEON DIVERS' CLUB
Wanna explore every dank dungeon in the kingdom? You can do it with the special field trips sponsored by this club.

LIVING CHESS CLUB
Compete with actual people as the pieces – bishops, rooks, knights, etc. <u>Fun for all ages</u>.

Didn't like it.

MAGIC DEBATE SOCIETY
Use your magic powers to make a point . . . or to clamp a magic mouth-plug on to your opponent's yapper.

Maybe you didn't like it because you can't actually play chess? :)

MECH CLUB
Gearheads and Mech Makers build and battle with their favourite mechs.

THE SQUIREBOTS

While the squires have always enjoyed being an important part of noble life in Knighton, their role has changed a lot as technology gets faster and smarter. The kingdom's inventors have designed a clever and hardworking service android, known as the squirebot. These skilled robots can do all the tasks currently performed by human squires. <u>Squirebots assist our knights, as well as handling all the everyday chores around the castle. The new squirebots are great at carrying out their duties and protecting the kingdom from threats at the same time</u>. I have asked our academy experts to put together a list of dos and don'ts for students to consider when dealing with androids.

They're great at holding up targets and running away screaming!

So they can mess them up – I'm talking about you, butterbot Dennis

SQUIREBOT DOS AND DON'TS

Any chore is a challenge.

DO
assign them all your <u>most challenging chores</u>.

DO
keep them properly charged and maintained.

I once met a squirebot with a pet toaster. He named him Gutsy.

How adorable! ;)

How tragic! What a waste of a good toaster. :P

DO
give them a compliment every so often – squirebots have <u>feelings</u> too.

DON'T
feed them sticky food, or <u>any food</u> for that matter. They're machines. They don't need nutrition.

DON'T
hit them with heavy objects, vehicles, or explosives.

DON'T
<u>laugh at them</u> if they fall over or look silly while carrying out their duties. Which happens often.

Oh, now I know why Axl is always cooking with Chef Éclair.

Our friendship runs deep.

As deep as your stomach, no doubt!

Oops. :)

TOP BOTS
OF KNIGHTON

1. ALICE SQUIRES

Knighton's most popular, on-air holo-vision personality. 'Queen of Happy Talk' Alice works on KNN, hosts infotainment spectacu-galas, as well as working the red carpet at Holowood premieres with CamBot, Riccardo. Alice's specialties include celebrity gossip, staring dreamily at famous actors and simply being FABULOUS!

2. FANCYPANTS

The King's rather proper, right-hand bot, FancyPants, pretty much runs the kingdom. He ensures the castle lights stay on, the hover-trains run, and the King does not destroy himself doing whatever it is he does all day. FancyPants believes the earth is shaped like a giant banana and is allergic to velvet rope.

3. ROBOT HOODLUM

Rumours abound about a once-faithful squirebot who has gone rogue and now hides out in a petrified forest on the edge of Knighton with his gang of 'Merry Mechs'. Legend has it that this outlaw bot robs from the rich so that he may help the poor and broken squirebots of the kingdom. But most people believe the 'Robot Hoodlum' is just a robot fairy tale.

4. CHEF ÉCLAIR

One of the kingdom's greatest culinary masters, <u>Chef Éclair</u> speaks with a French accent. Why does a robot have a French accent? Who knows? Perhaps he learned it while studying at Knighton's Culinary Academy with super-famous chef Gobbleton Rambley. Whatever his language is, there's only one word you need to know when he's around – YUM!

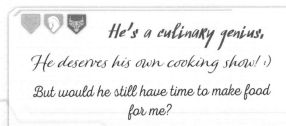

He's a culinary genius.

He deserves his own cooking show! :)

But would he still have time to make food for me?

I REMEMBER JESTRO BREAKING A SERVANTBOT.

Was his joke that bad?

IT WAS A RIDDLE. IT STARTED WITH: 'I ONLY LIE. I'VE NEVER, EVER SAID ANYTHING TRUE'.

But if what he said was true, that meant he wasn't lying.

It must have caused a loop in the bot's brain.

Mine as well. Thinking makes me hungry. :/

MISCELLANEOUS BOTS

These are not famous individuals, but they are some of the kingdom's most popular types of squirebots.

SERVANTBOTS
Let's give a big cheer for the good old basic servantbots. They are assigned to do anything requested of them by a master. At the academy, most of their tasks involve setting up absurdly dangerous stunts and then jumping frantically out of the way.

GUARDBOTS
Who protects our kingdom? Guardbots. That's who. The truth is, their battle skills are extremely limited. However, they are more proficient at getting randomly smashed by monsters, and/or running away screaming.

FARMERBOTS
OK, robots don't even eat food, so why do they run all the farms in the kingdom? Because no one else wants to! Plus, they not only plant and pick all the crops, but they also make excellent scarecrows. Just make sure the sprinklers aren't on when they're out in the fields or they'll rust solid.

HERALDBOTS

Knighton may be one of the most digital kingdoms around, but some things still need to be delivered by hand – robot hand, that is. Heraldbots race around as fast as their little legs will carry them with head-sirens blaring, to deliver news, packages and even takeaway food.

Can't fight on an empty stomach!

ACTORBOT

Yikes! Is that a Scurrier? No, it's just a squirebot in costume. So convincing! This is the actorbot class of droid – normal squirebots who perform in Knighton video and theatre productions. They're surprisingly good actors and have a big screen presence.

They do all their own stunts! Tell them to break a leg and they will! SNAP!

ENTERTAINERBOT

Much like an actorbot, this squirebot's duty is to perform for audiences across the realm. They sing, they dance, they tell jokes. Enjoy at your own risk.

I never actually like how they perform. Too stiff. Too ... machine-like.

PAST STUDENTS

KING EGGRED HALBERT

<u>His Majesty, <u>King Halbert</u></u>, is one of the Knights' Academy's most famous students. His father, King Thinneous 'the Nervous' Halbert II, worried about his son's future (he worried about almost everything). But after King Halbert attended the academy, the world was his oyster – his end of term project was about ancient mapmakers who used molluscs for navigational aids. Though he proved himself as a knight, it was really his kindness that got him recognized. He was always very thoughtful and good, and tried to make everything around him just and fair. (In fact, he organized the first 'Just and Fair Fair' while he was a student.)

I HOPE YOU KNELT BEFORE READING THIS PASSAGE – IT SHOWS PROPER RESPECT TO HIS HIGHNESS.

Do you kneel every time you read about the King in the papers too?

That would make reading a newspaper on the toilet pretty tough.

QUEEN HAMA HALBERT

Her Majesty, <u>Queen Hama Halbert</u>, entered the academy as a commoner. She quickly earned her title – 'the Kicker of Butts' – for her hard work on the training ground with her favoured weapon, the hammer. Boy could she kick butt. She was the first first-year student to be President of the Impact Instrument Club, and she was the lead striker for the Brickland Brick winning tournament teams, in the years 004, 005 and 006. She was also in the glee club and every tapestry-dying tournament in her final year.

That's my mum!
She's totally
amazing!

One day I hope
to become royal.

That's not really
how it works,
Lance.

SIR SWORDMORE BRICKLAND

Sir Brickland is not only this school's principal and the editor of this handbook, he is also the single most important figure in the history of this academy! [Editor's note: this is a completely true fact; no exaggeration]. The mighty Brickland began his career as a heroic, monster-fighting warrior, teaming with (future) King Halbert and (overrated) superstar <u>Ned Knightly.</u> Brickland's undeniable leadership skills led to an appointment as principal of the academy during what he calls, 'The Golden Age of Knight Schooling'. With the kingdom free of monsters and most major threats, the academy became a lightly attended and easily managed institution of relaxed – er, learning. For several decades, the academy only graduated a few students a year, allowing Brickland plenty of free time to work on his second career as a minstrel playwright.

Hey!
Ned Knightly was definitely NOT overrated. He was the coolest Knightonian ever and a total legend.

Sorry, Macy. That title has now been taken (hint: by me).

YOU played HIM in a film, not the other way around. Your opinion is invalid.

Ha! So you did watch it! :P

NED KNIGHTLY

One of the most famous knights to ever graduate from the Knights' Academy, Knightly went on to star in several bestselling comic books, feature films, and 5-D holographic epics. But as Principal Brickland (editor of this handbook) explains: 'I went to school with Ned Knightly and Ned Knightly . . . was no Ned Knightly'. In other words, the real Ned fell a few gauntlets short of his full-fisted legend. This 'hero of heroes' just had a really good publicist. He spent a lot more time at school gardening and practising his Dutch clogging skills than honing his warrior abilities. In fact, during The Great Battle at the Golden Castle, Ned was in the latrine, leaving the REAL heroics to the Mighty Brickland. [Editor's note: still not exaggerating]. Ned's brother, <u>Jokes Knightly</u>, is far more noble and entertaining.

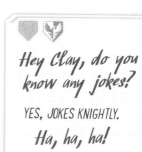

Hey Clay, do you know any jokes?

YES, JOKES KNIGHTLY.

Ha, ha, ha!

OTHER FAMOUS PAST STUDENTS

Over the years, the Knights' Academy has had many, many famous graduates. (In some cases, when we say 'famous', we mean 'infamous'.) Here is <u>a sample of some of them</u>:

JORAH TIGHTWAD – One of the richest, fattest and most big-headed men in the kingdom, 'The One Who Doesn't Spend a Penny' became famous for finishing leftover food from other students' plates.

SIR GRIFFITHS – His best friend at the academy is now the Principal (Brickland). Though he went on to become a famously brave and honourable knight, while at the academy, he and 'Binky' Brickland accumulated more black marks than any other students.

JURGEN VON STROHEIM – Now a famous film director, Jurgen Von Stroheim began his career as a knight and graduate of the academy. But he was better with a camera than he was with a sword and became much more deadly in the editing room than on the training grounds.

JOKES KNIGHTLY – With a disarming sense of humour, many thought Jokes made the academy a more fun place. Others thought his dumb puns and stupid knock-knock jokes made life at the academy intolerable. He decided he liked making laughs more than being chivalrous, so he became a comedian.

BRICKNEY SPEARS – Famous for her singing and spear work at the academy, Brickney Spears went on to become a well-known pop star in Knighton. Her moves with a spear are great . . . but only in rehearsal. In real combat, she's in trouble.

CONCLUSIONS

The end of the beginning? The what of the what? Brickland's like the riddle-master!

Now do you understand how hard it is to become a knight? All you've done is read part of a book! Sure, it's an important book, and there will be many tests and quizzes about it, but this isn't even <u>the end of the beginning</u>!

What do you do now? Find a grindstone and put your nose on it. All night if you have to, and all day as well. The best advice I can give you right now is summed up in one word: WORK. HARD. OK, so that's two words, but stop editing the editor and WORK HARD. You understand me, squire? Read over this section again. I sense a <u>surprise test</u> coming tomorrow . . .

Your hard-working principal setting a shining example,

Sir Swordmore Brickland

TESTS ARE IMPORTANT. THEY KEEP YOU SHARP. LIKE A SWORD, ONLY FOR YOUR BRAIN. I LIKE HAVING A SHARP SWORD-BRAIN.

Read, read, read. There are sooo many better ways to spend your time. I always paid people to read for me.

Now, THIS is what it's all about!

So, who's uploading first?

HE WHO STARTED IT ALL, OUR WIZARD PROTECTOR – MERLOK 2.0.

I prefer to call him our Shield of Schooling and Protection ;)

THE KNIGHT'S CODE: DIGITAL EDITION

WHEN POWERS GET DIGITAL

BY MERLOK 2.0

Merlok 2.0 here, to um, er . . . to talk about what us digital wizards (well that's just me really) refer to as the 'digital age' of knighthood. It appears that monsters have returned to Knighton, so the time has come for us to use more than the usual swords and shields to protect our kingdom – the time has come for us to use . . . <u>NEXO Powers</u>. Oh my, that sounded so dramatic.

What are NEXO Powers, you ask? Well, er, let me start by <u>revealing some of the secrets</u> of my high-tech amazingness . . .

Yoohoo!

It's not that much of a mystery! – Ava

NEXO Powers allow me to download all sorts of incredible powers that are stored in my digital, magical memory. Right yes, OK, I know you're waiting for me to say something wise and magical. So, here goes: young knights-in-training, learn everything you can about how to use your NEXO Powers. It will serve you well in defending the kingdom of Knighton.

Now, I shall go into a bit more detail . . .

And so will the great vehicles that I made – Robin

Congrats on your first digi sticky note, Robin!

I used to just like bashing stuff, but NEXO Powers are very cool. I can't really function without them now.

NEXO POWERS ARE COOL INDEED, BUT WE NEED TO MAKE SURE WE REMEMBER THE LESSONS OF THE PAST AND MIX THEM WITH THE TECHNOLOGY OF THE FUTURE.

Oh, barf! Why do you always have to be the uptight knight? 'Embrace the future,' I say.

NEXO POWERS
BY MERLOK 2.0

It has to be said that the single greatest advancement in the conduct and performance of a knight's duty has been the introduction of <u>NEXO Powers</u>.

NEXO Powers are a type of um . . . er . . . magical enhancement to a knight's combat skills. In the past, such powers were provided by potions, spells and talismans . . . oh, those were such magical times . . . but I digress, so let me get back to the point . . . these new upgrades can now be wirelessly downloaded in a digital form.

You can receive these digital downloads to your shields or other gear. Receiving one will provide you with a variety of extraordinary powers such as: the Anvil of Trouble, Banana Bombs, Bubble Gum Misfire (my personal favourite), Chicken Power, Funky Fungus and many, many more. Downloads are essential for battling the many new and exceptionally powerful monsters that have afflicted the kingdom of late. But to be honest, most people <u>don't actually understand how NEXO Powers work</u>.

To help explain this further, I have turned to one of the kingdom's main experts in this discipline, who also just happens to be our technological wonder child here on the Fortrex . . . <u>Ava Prentis</u>.

Wooohooo! NEXO Powers rule!

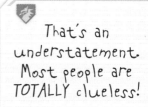

That's an understatement. Most people are TOTALLY clueless!

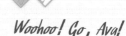

Woohoo! Go, Ava!

You got this one. Show 'em how it's done!

NEXO Power + girl power = AWESOME!

HOW NEXO POWERS WORK
BY AVA PRENTIS

So, I know that everyone who has one of these books pastes digital sticky notes all over it. So I'm just going to give you <u>a little space to get that out of your system</u>. Here goes . . .

Uh . . .
Sorry, Ava, I'm not sure what to write.

Yeah, now that you WANT us to make fun of your page, it's not really much . . . fun . . . any more.

You go, girl! You totally shut down those doodling doofuses!

CARRY ON, AVA. YOU ARE WISE BEYOND YOUR YEARS.

Uh, can I still draw a moustache on her picture?

Now that you've had your creative freedom, I think we can get down to business (nice moustache by the way – I assume you've marked up my picture as well). Anyway . . . the concept behind NEXO Powers is simple enough. But first, you have to understand a little bit about the nature of magic. To be blunt, there's no great 'magic' about magic. <u>Doing magic means using special words, hand signs and pictures to make extraordinary things happen. Spells contain many magic words. And spells are just another form of data – information that can be processed by a machine. Once this data is entered into a computer system, it can be processed, changed and then sent to an end user.</u> You, the knight, are the end user.

It's kind of like sending a picture of a flower from your computer to your printer. The power and beauty of the flower remains intact regardless of what form it takes, whether it's lighting up your screen, or hanging on your wall as a piece of paper. It's the same with <u>spells and magic</u>.

Whoaa . . . She's makin' my head spin.

PAY ATTENTION. YOU'LL LEARN SOMETHING.

Maybe . . .

I get hungry when I'm confused. Cupcakes! Yum!

And cupcakes!

Again with the understatement.

Yes! I see the word 'battle.' Now that I understand.

I love how Ava makes something like 'data entry' sound exciting.

But like any kind of new technology, there are <u>glitches and quirks in both the input and output systems</u>. For starters, one has to get the initial 'magic' data into the system. It's possible to type or scan some forms of magic into a modern NEXO KNIGHTS hero's system. But the way our system got its first data was the result of a fierce, old-fashioned magical <u>battle</u> between Merlok and the powerful Book of Monsters in Merlok's Library at the king's castle. The conflict ended in a massive, magical explosion that destroyed most of the library. It also accidentally sent Merlok, and all of his magical energy, into the castle's computer system.

Another way of putting it is this: this magical explosion was the most important <u>'Act of Data Entry'</u> that the world has ever known. The castle's computer now contained all the spells and energy of the most powerful wizard in the kingdom. With a few tweaks here and there, our team was able to turn this magical energy into the NEXO Powers now used by the Knights.

I'm just giving you a <u>simple, technical</u> explanation. Merlok is now literally inside the computers we use on our rolling castle – the Fortrex. He exists in a digital form we call Merlok 2.0. He helps run our castle and our gear, as well as giving out his powerful digital magic when needed. It is not a perfect system. We may be dealing with a type of magic here, but that doesn't mean the way it is used is always magical.

For now, just be aware that digital magic is here to help you and your kingdom. Study this book and practise its recommendations, and you too will one day be a great NEXO KNIGHTS hero. Or, if you're really smart, you can come and work in the Fortrex Command Centre with me. I'll show you something REALLY exciting – <u>lines and lines of computer code</u>!

Did she just use the word 'simple'?

I think I need another cupcake.

Chasing monsters: boooring. Riding a hovershield: exciting. Watching lines of computer code: REALLY exciting! Go, AVA!

SHIELDS
BY AVA PRENTIS

I also use mine for Flying! Woohoo!

My shield makes me look really cool! The light bounces off it to perfectly light up my strong, leading-man features.

UGHHH . . . GIVE ME A BREAK. IT'S NOT A BEAUTY PRODUCT. IT'S FOR COMBAT!

A shield is possibly the most important tool used by a NEXO KNIGHTS hero <u>in his or her battle against evil</u>. Modern NEXO KNIGHTS' shields can receive powerful digi-magic downloads and this is what makes them so special. Each shield is made of rare metals with receptor strips stuck in it. These allow the shield to attract and process the downloads. The shield then <u>sends this amazing magic power to the rest of the armour and weapons used by the knight</u>.

Students at the academy will be provided with what is known as the <u>Student Shield</u> – a slightly smaller version of the traditional shield. Once a student's training is complete at the academy, <u>he or she will receive an official Knight's Shield of the Realm at their graduation ceremony</u>. Thus, they become SHIELD BEARERS.

Below is a sample of some existing NEXO KNIGHTS' shields.

**Logging off,
Ava Prentis
Knights' Academy Apprentice**

CLAY'S SHIELD

*'Student shield'?
More like
'Baby shield'.*

Unless your dad (the king) won't let you have one.

Sorry about getting cupcake icing everywhere!

NOTE THE NOBLE FALCON ON MY SHIELD.
IT STANDS FOR HONOUR, JUSTICE AND COURAGE.

*Or . . . maybe it just means you're a birdbrain!
Ha, ha, ha, ha!*

My shield has the mighty horse. It represents all that is me – strong, handsome and ready to race!

UGH . . .
I THINK IT JUST MEANS YOU'RE A BEAST OF BURDEN.

LANCE'S SHIELD

Check out the fox, dudes! Just like my last name – Aaron Fox! Oh, and I rigged my shield so it can fly and hover. Why? Because it's AWESOME!

AARON'S SHIELD

MACY'S SHIELD

It took a while, but I finally got my mother's old shield - Dragon Fire. And, yes, it's a little pink. But if you EVER make fun of it, you'll feel its burn!

I THINK YOUR SHIELD'S AMAZING, MACY. AND WELL-DESERVED.

Oh, you're such a suck-up, birdbrain.

AXL'S SHIELD

My shield has a bull on it. Most people think this represents strength. I think it represents . . . beef products!

Yum!

THE BEST POWERS
BY MERLOK 2.0

Indeed :)
Well, maybe a little.

So, now you know how it all really works. I expect Ava would have probably explained it better, but anyway . . . it is time to present the best of the best powers. NEXOOOO KNIGHTS!

This reminds me of something . . . that's it! It smells like Whiparella's Toxic Perfume!

Peweeeew!

Sour Strike: you leave a poisonous trail behind yourself.

Fist Smash: five giant fists come down from the sky one after the other, and pound your enemies.

THIS IS MY FAVOURITE, NEXT TO GLORY OF KNIGHTON AND THE CHAMPION OF CHIVALRY.

Power of United Knights: call out for one of your fellow knights to help you in battle.

Magnetize: a mystic energy that violently pulls all enemies together.

Bonkers Beans: turn your enemies crazy with these barmy jelly beans.

Draining Scarf: you entangle enemies with scarves and mummify them.

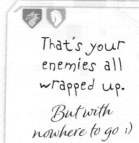

That's your enemies all wrapped up.

But with nowhere to go :)

Chicken Power: smash and distract your enemies with eggs falling from the sky.

Rock and Roll: hear a guitar riff with every strike.

Bwammmm!

Mech Master: summon your squirebot to help you in battle.

Bubble Gum Misfire: you create a bubblegum sphere around yourself.

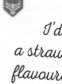

I'd like a strawberry-flavoured one, please.

HQ AND VEHICLES
BY ROBIN UNDERWOOD

I do enjoy some quality time in the lounge the most.

You're not supposed to be lounging all the time, Lance.

I woulda said it was super, super cool. I like the word cool. And super.

IT MEETS MY HIGH STANDARDS FOR A BATTLE-TRAINING FACILITY.

Oh, I think I've left a soufflé in the oven.

So, what's the problem with a castle? It just sits there waiting to be attacked, that's what. But the Fortrex? Well, it's a completely cool, powered, rolling fortress. It's got everything a NEXO KNIGHTS hero needs: a place to sleep, a command centre, a garage, an armoury, a holo training room, a kitchen and a lounge. All this and big tank treads, too. Like, REALLY big. Bet you wish you had one, huh?

THE FORTREX
OUTSIDE VIEW

Power Lines – running throughout the Fortrex.

The Parapet – the place where you can look out over the countryside, or where you can fire at monsters.

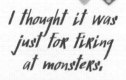

I thought it was just for firing at monsters.

I thought it was just for looking out over the countryside :)

The Bowtrex – a big crossbow on top of the Fortrex that can launch all sorts of things (including squirebots).

Hologram Banners – these can display almost anything and are holographic.

We should display some of my selfies in our next battle!

Defence Towers – for 'towering' over monsters and dropping stuff on their heads.

View Screen Shield – on the front of the Fortrex so folk inside can talk to people outside.

Blasters – for blasting back bad guys at close range.

Drawbridge Door – the main door of the Fortrex. (It helps with getting in and getting out.)

THE FORTREX
IN ACTION!

The blasters fire automatically if bad guys get too close.

WHAM!
Ol' Burnzie ge'
'draw-bridged!' F
pickings for A>

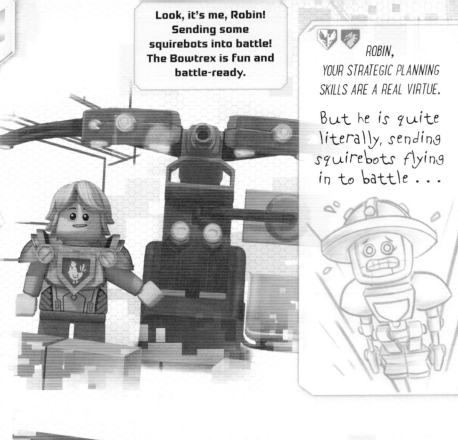

Look, it's me, Robin! Sending some squirebots into battle! The Bowtrex is fun and battle-ready.

ROBIN, YOUR STRATEGIC PLANNING SKILLS ARE A REAL VIRTUE.

But he is quite literally, sending squirebots flying in to battle . . .

Chef Éclair gets in on the action . . . in the most delicious way.

It's a long (and delicious) way down to the pit of my stomach :D

COMMAND CENTRE

THIS IS WHERE IT ALL HAPPENS AND WHERE THE GANG HANGS OUT, CRUSHING DIGITS AND THE LIKE.

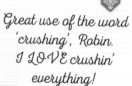

Great use of the word 'crushing', Robin. I LOVE crushin' everything!

My workstation is very utilitarian. Because it's a workstation.

Side note: Merlok 2.0 can download almost any song you could ever want.

Never thought my dad's motorized caravan would be completely computerized. He's not so into the high-tech stuff.

This place is like something out of a cheesy sci-fi holovision show. I would have used more gold in its design.

119

KNIGHTS' QUARTERS
EVERYONE NEEDS SOME ZZZZ TIME

Sleeping.
It's what I live for.
When I'm awake?
Well then I'd mostly
like to take a nap.

Is this room
empty? Oh no,
wait-it's just
Clay's room :P

Hey, Clay! You
should tidy up!

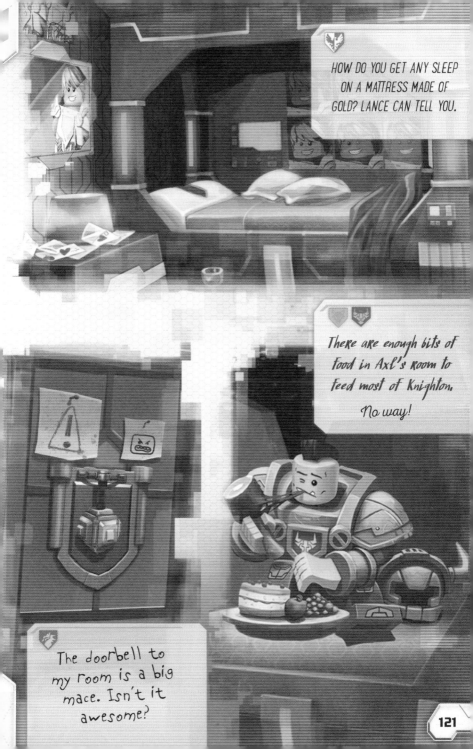

THE HOLO-
TRAINING AREA
PRETTY GREAT, HUH?

This place can simulate anywhere we want.

Can it simulate a cafeteria?

I TAKE A BREAK FROM TRAINING ON THE WEEKENDS. OK, I DON'T REALLY.

THE BEST SEQUENCE IS: THRUST, PARRY, PARRY, THRUST, JUMP BACK, SMILE, REPEAT.

ARMOURY
EVERY KIND OF WEAPON YOU CAN IMAGINE.

Ah, I always feel at home here.

You know how Aaron ties his shoes? In little bows. Get it?

I GET IT :)

Mum always said, 'Never come between a knight and their axe'.

KITCHEN AND DINING ROOM
OTHERWISE KNOWN AS AXL'S HQ.

The eating happens here.

Technically your eating happens everywhere!

CHEF ÉCLAIR KEEPS THE KITCHEN VERY NEAT. BUT YOU NEED TO BREAK SOME EGGS TO MAKE AN OMELETTE.

Those pans are potential weapons. They look like flattened maces :)

THE LOUNGE
TIME TO RELAX!

Ah . . . Time for some . . . lounging.

YOU SHOULDN'T SPEND MUCH TIME HERE. UNLESS YOU'RE WATCHING SOME TUTORIALS.

My secret move? Grab a snack, a Lancetastic Soda, then the comfy chair before anyone else does.

This is the comfiest chair – tell no one!

Aaron is the best video-game player in the Fortrex. Well, except for Axl. Oh, and Clay. And Robin and Ava too.

THE ENGINE
IT'S BIG, LOUD AND HYPERCHARGED!

Everything here is top secret; so don't tell anyone you saw it. Even me.

TOO LATE, ROBIN, WE SAW IT. :D

Six-speed transmission.

Is it fast or slow?

We can get about 50,000 hover horsepower out of this baby.

Gotta change the oil every 5,000 miles.

THE GARAGE

WHERE ALL THE COOL STUFF IS CREATED.

This is the place where I built the Minitrex and the Ultra Armour as well as my Black Knight Mech.

ALL THE VEHICLES GET PARKED HERE.

Very informative Clay. If you hadn't said that we would never have known where to park them. ;)

Wanna see how fast I can change a set of tyres or treads?

Should we watch it in slow-mo?

There are about a gazillion screwdrivers in here.

RUMBLE BLADE
BY CLAY MOORINGTON

Built like a <u>giant Claymore Sword</u>, the Rumble Blade is cutting edge in its design and extremely fast. There are two side-cycles that detach and are strong enough to hold someone even as big as Axl. The central sword portion shoots off and becomes a jet-powered flyer, which is perfect for surprising unsuspecting monsters. My Rumble Blade has the perfect service history. That way, I know it is always in impeccable shape and ready for anything.

Wouldn't it be great to have a real sword this big?

Hey, Mr Gadget, why don't you just make one?

Could Axl really fit on this?

The Rumble Blade has extra energy shooters for anyone sneaking up from behind.

The cockpit gives me great driving visibility.

Must remember never to sneak up on Clay!

BOW FLYER
BY AARON FOX

Does Aaron ever bow out of a battle?

He doesn't, especially when monsters cross his bows :)

Dude, my Bow Flyer can rain down digi-arrows on monsters!

Woohoo! Let's take to the skies on my flying <u>bow</u> blaster. How cool is this thing? Way cool! It's like a giant bow, only it flies and can shoot energy arrows. There's nothing like takin' down targets or monsters from some altitude.

I'm thinking of repainting it neon green. What do you think?

Always better
to be above the
action, right?

HEY, THOSE CHAINS REMIND
ME OF BEAST MASTER.

Beast Master?!
Where?

Sometimes I like to cut
the engines and see how
far I can glide.

THUNDER MACE

BY MACY HALBERT

I like to call my vehicle the '**Mace Masher**'. That's completely unofficial – don't tell my dad, the king – he's totally into making sure everything is official. It's tough, rugged, and it can mash like the biggest mace you've ever seen. Everything a girl wants in a vehicle.

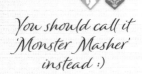

You should call it 'Monster Masher' instead :)

Mmmm, mashed potatoes. I'm so hungry.

Look! My vehicle has a giant, spinning mace!

MACY, WHEN YOU THUNDER PAST THE MONSTERS ON THAT THING, THEY HAVE FACES LIKE THUNDER.

Wow, Clay. You're a real joke masher :)

Extra-wide tyres for grinding across the battlefield.

MECHA HORSE
BY LANCE RICHMOND

Really?

I have the <u>classiest vehicle of all the Knights</u>. It's a classic hover horse named Concordo that converts into a super cycle at the touch of a button. A stylish knight like me requires nothing less. I don't know how it actually works, I just drive around looking good in it. My <u>Mecha Horse</u> is the best because, well, I'm the best. Obviously.

It's a Mecha Horse, it's a cycle . . . it's two vehicles in one!

IF YOU CONVERT IT INTO A HORSE, YOU CAN LOOK JUST LIKE A KNIGHT FROM THE PAST.

Yeah, it's perfect if you happen to be starring in historical movies! ;)

The steering controls are solid gold.

LANCE MAKES DENNIS POLISH THEM EVERY DAY!

I shine too as I cruise along, and my hair looks great with the wind rushing through it. (Not too much though . . . I may have to go out later.)

TOWER CARRIER
BY AXL

BRICK: How about, 'Be Ready, I Come Keenly'?

Six wheels of ground-poundin' power. Wide and low to the ground for huggin' the road. That part in the back is called the <u>BRICK</u>: Book Repository Integral Containment Keeper. Robin thought up the name and built it in case we ever captured a magic book. That way, there's a safe place to transport it. It's totally awesome!

I customized the seat so my bottom never gets tired.

The BRICK is fully detachable if we need to hide it somewhere.

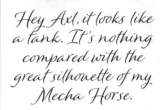

Hey Axl, it looks like a tank. It's nothing compared with the great silhouette of my Mecha Horse.

Yeah, can you tell us which part is the front and which is the back?

You may laugh, but my Tower Carrier is like a surprise waiting to jump out of a giant cake.

Changing six tyres takes a lot of time. And with squirebots helping, it takes twice as long!

THE BLACK KNIGHT
BY ROBIN UNDERWOOD

Sounds awesome! I can totally tutor you in 'not doing anything' if you need me to.

The life of a first-year student is not cool. All I hear is: '<u>Robin, you can't do this' and 'Robin, you can't do that</u>'. 'You're too young to fight the monsters' and 'You're too young to scan the powers'.

So, if everyone's telling you not to do stuff, what *can* you do to wipe out monsters in the battle against evil? You design cool stuff that can do the job for you! Take a look at my Black Knight – a fully equipped, high-tech mech! Pretty cool, huh? Monsters don't stand a chance against this giant knight, complete with jet-powered boots, gigantic sword and <u>arrow shooter</u>.

And you know what the most awesome thing about it is? Its ability to hack into the Fortrex for NEXO Power downloads. What's that you say, 'You're too young to scan the powers, Robin'? If you did, I didn't hear you! :D

That did say 'arrow shooter', right?

Ava, can you code that so that Merlok can't read it?

138

No kidding! The Black Knight totally saved the kingdom when Jestro disguised all his monsters as us!

PRINCIPAL BRICKLAND BANNED IT FROM THE KNIGHTS' ACADEMY CAMPUS. AND SNEAKING OUT TO OPERATE IT – EVEN IF IT IS TO SAVE THE KINGDOM – IS STRICTLY PROHIBITED.

I can totally be Robin's 'breaking the rules' tutor, if he needs one.

WEAPONS
BY MERLOK 2.0

OBVIOUSLY THE SWORD IS THE BEST WEAPON FOR EVERY SITUATION.

I prefer lots of mashing. Um, I mean macing.

Boo-yah . . . the bow is the only way to go. That rhymes, you know!

I prefer the axe. Well, my name is Axl . . . so it's hardly surprising, is it?

A lance is the weapon of a gentleman and a Richmond. Which is why I'm the only one who can wield it with such grace, elegance and style.

It's me again (Merlok 2.0, digital wizard and all that). I'm here to . . . what was it again? Oh yes, that's it . . . I'm here to introduce this section on <u>advanced weapons</u>. It has often been said that a NEXO KNIGHTS hero's greatest weapon is their mind. Of course, that is if it is a sharp mind! Ha, ha, I said 'sharp mind'. Get it? Sharp weapon. Sharp mind . . . Never mind . . . Well, anyway, sometimes you just need to hit something really hard with some heavy stone and steel – and some NEXO Powers too. For these occasions, personal weapons should be used.

You have a wide range of amazing, high-tech weapons at your disposal. Of course, each of you will choose what you like best or what works best for you when battling monsters. For example, originally, Lance tried to use a bow, but he was hopeless with it, so he discovered that a lance was the weapon for him. It's quite obvious if you think about it? Isn't it? So long as the weapon can channel NEXO Powers – which all advanced weapons can – you can choose it for battle.

CLAYMORE SWORD

BY CLAY MOORINGTON

As our mentor Merlok 2.0 said, knights have a wide range of amazing, high-tech weapons to choose from. My choice is a sword. It is the most classic weapon, used by many of the famous knights of Knighton.

The Claymore Sword is a broadsword, which delivers a powerful attack. It can be swung with one hand, but due to its massive size, it is extremely heavy.

Wow, Clay, you're posing so heroically :)

The sword is very sharp. Do not point it at yourself or you'll poke your eye out.

The blade is made of imperial steel from the south coast of Knighton. This is the strongest known metal in the kingdom.

Ridges carved into the blade provide high-speed transport channels for energy.

Internal core in cross guard offers unlimited storage capacity for NEXO Power downloads.

Handle grip is wrapped in wolf leather or gryphon skin.

Pommel is best for cracking walnuts, but don't ever let Clay see you use it for that.

SIZE COMPARISON

CLAYMORE SWORD   NORMAL SWORD

My lance is even bigger. And shinier.

143

BLAZER BOW
BY AARON FOX

Yeah, I tried this one and I must say it's overrated.

A bad workman always blames his tools.

I would never blame my tools. They are sooo cool.

Want to defeat monsters and be quick about it? My <u>crossbow</u> can fire an almost infinite supply of digi-arrows – a highly charged, shaft-like burst of energy. Wow! Can you feel the power? Oh, yeah! Bows are the grooviest weapons in Knighton, so if you need to strike at a monster from any kind of distance, you know what to choose. Combined with hover-shield riding, the Blazer Bow is the best of the best, dude!

Muzzle coated in liquid Spurion to enhance speed and force of digi-arrows.

Look at those limbs – they're made of flexitech and are nearly unbreakable. Out of this world!

Barrel holds and produces up to 70 digi-arrows per minute. Great result, huh?

ACTUALLY, THEY ARE NOT OUT OF THIS WORLD. THEY ARE CARVED FROM A SYNTHETIC MATERIAL THAT NOW GROWS WILD IN THE FORESTS OF KNIGHTON.

Only a small squeeze of a pistol grip and you rapid-fire a rain of digi-arrows. Monsters, beware!

Are you serious, Clay?

I'm afraid he is. :D

THE LANCE
BY LANCE RICHMOND

If you want your weapon to not only be effective but striking as well, choose the lance. Of course, yours won't be as glamorous as mine (it's a Richmond's lance) but it will definitely be better than any bow.

My lance is both lightweight and strong. And it's elegant, just like me! Robin told me it has an <u>internal carton</u> providing high-speed processing of energy normally not seen in weapons of this type. You see, Aaron, not only your bow bursts energy!

It has an internal CARBON nanotube spine, man! Will you ever learn? :(

Never mind, I still look nifty with it.

Hey Lance, sQuiReRazzi!

Where?

I was kidding. But you're striking when you strike a pose! ;P

> The spear tip is shiny and elegant. Oh, and it also regulates the release of NEXO Power.

But you're still trying to use it for picking my nose, Not funny!

> The spear part extends more than three metres so I can pick a monster directly from my hammock.

Could you please pick me up a sausage too?

> Don't tell anyone, but there's a secret pocket inside the handle.

For carrying spare change and fan mail no doubt! :)

PHOTON MACE
BY MACY HALBERT

I must admit, your mace has a surprising elegance and charm.

Thanks, Lance, I know that was hard for you to admit.

Some narrow-minded people say that weapons aren't really for girls. They are sooo wrong! What about Joan of Dark or Catherine of Dragon? They wielded their weapons with such grace. My mum, Queen Halbert, who comes from a long line of mace-wielding warriors, gave me my beloved <u>Photon Mace</u>. Why is it called a Photon Mace? Well, put simply, it packs the power of the sun when I swing it! Look out, monsters, here I come!

Head carved from solarantium stone – an extremely rare and indestructible material that is believed to have originated on the surface of the sun.

So, can we call you a Sun Warrior, Macy?

Yeah, you'd better grab a shield and some SPF 50 when I'm in action!

Handle is made from the silicon-infused tusk of an angry woolly mammoth. And if you've ever tried to get a bunch of silicon into an angry mammoth's tusk, you'd be really impressed by that.

I THOUGHT THAT MAMMOTHS WERE EXTINCT . . .

Spare energy is stored in a special reservoir at the base of the handle, so I have a secret pocket too.

BIG POWER AXE
BY AXL

Errr, what can I say? A weapon is a weapon. It should be practical and deliver <u>devastating strikes</u>. My axe was forged from resources found only in my land: hyper-iron from the Deep Earth mines and wood from the Old Growth Ironwood Tree. It is strong and big just like me. North Hill Country, <u>I miss you so much</u>. :'(

Strikes to monsters or to fried chickens? :D

So big and so sensitive, oh . . .

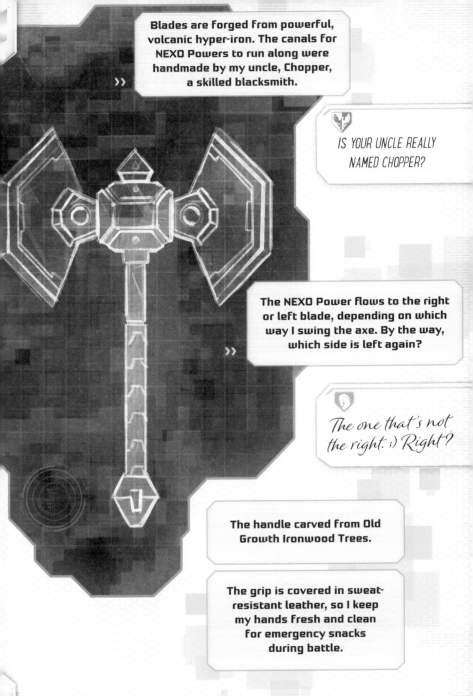

Blades are forged from powerful, volcanic hyper-iron. The canals for NEXO Powers to run along were handmade by my uncle, Chopper, a skilled blacksmith.

IS YOUR UNCLE REALLY NAMED CHOPPER?

The NEXO Power flows to the right or left blade, depending on which way I swing the axe. By the way, which side is left again?

The one that's not the right. ;) Right?

The handle carved from Old Growth Ironwood Trees.

The grip is covered in sweat-resistant leather, so I keep my hands fresh and clean for emergency snacks during battle.

JESTRO AND THE BOOK OF MONSTERS

BY MERLOK 2.0

So, you have great weapons, now you need some worthy enemies, right? Meet grumpy Jestro and the Book of Monsters. Odd couples don't get more odd or evil than this former royal jester <u>and his magical minion</u>. The Book of Monsters seems like he's really calling the shots, but then again he can't go anywhere other than the local library without his jokey companion.

Why didn't he like my place? I don't know . . . Maybe it was because I didn't let him take over the kingdom and I put him up on a dusty shelf . . . Well, now he's free with a little help from Jestro. They're two crazy guys trying to lead a team of Lava, Forest and Sea Monsters. But we are ready, aren't we, NEXO KNIGHTS team! Erm . . . <u>aren't we?</u>

'Magical minion'! Ha, ha, ha!

If the Book of Monsters heard that, he would need to eat the Knight's Book of Calm.

I didn't know that book existed . . . Does it exist?

Yes, Merlok, we are!

FOR THE KINGDOM!

LAVA MONSTERS

Don't forget Lava Beetle, Fire Scorpion and Storm Eye.

Yeah, they Rock! (Lava Rock.)

'**H**ot, nasty, fiery and really unfriendly' pretty much sums up the Lava Monsters faced by our team. There are generals like Magmar, and lieutenants like Beast Master and Lavaria. Then there are the common, everyday Magma Monsters: Scurriers, Globlins and Bloblins who'll melt you just like the others. <u>Too many to remember?</u> Just take a look around and search for something red and stinky.

Hey, what's the difference between a Globlin and a rolling lava rock?

None. Ha, ha, ha!

LAVARIA – JESTRO'S CHIEF SPY AND MISTRESS OF DISGUISE.

She has a hot temper!

Whiparella - she can spread fear with a SNAP of her nasty whips.

You know I'm Fearless, Erm . . . almost.

You know that one of Monster Master's Globlins is named Muffin? Sweet . . .

DON'T EVER TRY TO EAT HIM, AXL.

Too late ;)

SEA MONSTERS

Was that all too hot for you? It's time to cool down a bit with the cold and wet <u>Sea Monsters</u>. It's always best to be aware of them if you're near any type of water. If you're out at sea, look for pirate ships fuelled by electric eels. If you're staying on an island, you'd better check whether it has tentacles beneath it as well as palm trees on top. If you're crossing a moat . . . um, what was this one again? Oh yes, that's right. If you're crossing a moat, be sure to look down so that Sharkerado doesn't surprise you! That reminds me . . . Robin, we need to talk about water-resistant armour for the Knights.

I always wanted to meet Chef Savage and read his Cookbook of Evil.

Must chefs always have a French surname?

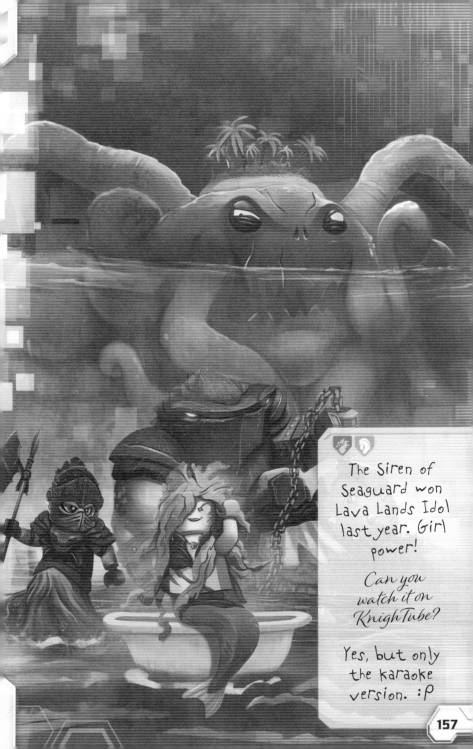

The Siren of Seaguard won Lava Lands Idol last year. Girl power!

Can you watch it on KnighTube?

Yes, but only the karaoke version. :P

157

FOREST MONSTERS

Being close to nature is something I would not recommend when in the presence of the Forest Monsters. A close hug from Bramblina or a bite of a poisoned apple from Baron Badwood will soon make you wish you had stayed at home. Achoo! Yikes, is that <u>my allergy</u> from the Strom of Spores made by Mushlord the Marauder? Heeelp!

Merlok, you are a hologram now . . .

Do I smell Baron 'Stinky' Badwood?

I just smell my cheese . . . you want a bite?

THE EVIL MOBILE

It's kinda nutty, but the Evil Mobile is faster than it looks.

As they say in the fashion news, it's hot, hot, hot!

WE MUST STUDY THIS VEHICLE AND KNOW OUR ENEMY.

Wow. Did you really just say, 'know our enemy'? I think you need a rewrite!

Even bad guys need a good ride, and Jestro has one – <u>the Evil Mobile</u>. It's big, bad and a bit of a mess, really. But that's what happens when you have Beast Master and his Chaos Monsters build you <u>a vehicle</u>.

How do you recognize it? Well, it looks just like Jestro. It has a jester's hat and jaws with enormous teeth. And huge wheels. And a catapult to launch lava rocks. And a movable cockpit . . . You get the idea.

And it's pulled by Burnzie and Sparkks, so it gets at least two monsters to the mile. Also, Globlins jump in and power the wheels when they need a bit of a boost.

Those guys must get hungry pulling that thing everywhere.

It's not very high-tech. Actually, it's not high-tech at all.

And it's got no air conditioning.

These Goblin-throwing catapults are dangerous. I know all too well!

Lava-rock wheels make for a bumpy ride.

I'm glad it doesn't fly.

TRACKING MONSTERS

One of the most important skills you must learn is how to track down the monsters threatening the security of our kingdom. Of course, you can find them in the Book of Monsters. But when released, all evil creatures leave different trails. Here's how to identify and track the markings of these dangerous foes.

SCURRIERS
The rodents of the monster world. Their footprints are small but very stinky. Scurriers are prone to distraction so they rarely walk in a straight line.

Ahhh, their feet are so tiny.

Oh, rodents. I always wanted to have a guinea pig :)

Let's play ball!

GLOBLINS

Globlins don't actually have feet so it's hard to find their footprints. But they still leave a trail – sort of like a beach ball made of lava bouncing across the countryside.

I never know if it's a monster or if it's Axl playing ducks and drakes.

UNDERWATER MONSTERS

Some monsters never surface. If you see ripples in the water, avoid diving in.

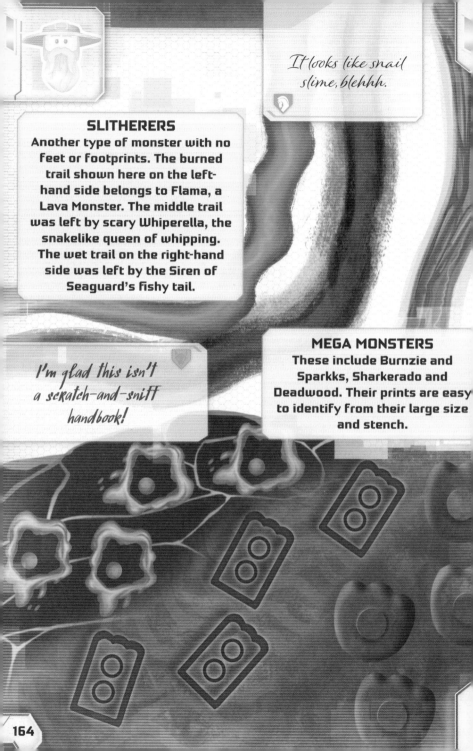

It looks like snail slime, blehhh.

SLITHERERS

Another type of monster with no feet or footprints. The burned trail shown here on the left-hand side belongs to Flama, a Lava Monster. The middle trail was left by scary Whiperella, the snakelike queen of whipping. The wet trail on the right-hand side was left by the Siren of Seaguard's fishy tail.

I'm glad this isn't a scratch-and-sniff handbook!

MEGA MONSTERS

These include Burnzie and Sparkks, Sharkerado and Deadwood. Their prints are easy to identify from their large size and stench.

MONSTER IN DISGUISE

These may look like dog prints, but they are actually the prints of Lavaria, who not only disguises her body, but her footprints as well.

Hey, did anyone ever find that lost dog? Oh wait . . . It's Lavaria.

OTHER MONSTERS

Most normal monsters will leave a footprint similar to a human, but with burned, wet or muddy edges.

Are there ANY normal monsters?

FIGHTING TIPS

BY CLAY MOORINGTON

That's a fancy way of saying, 'You mess with us and we'll go all "medieval" on you!'

A knight's goal in combat is never to cause unnecessary harm or suffering to an opponent. A good knight just wants to <u>seem strong and brave enough to put anyone off from attacking the kingdom</u>. There are many ways to seem strong and brave.
Below is a list.

The best defence is a strong attack, right guys?

Scare them away! I can do that.

1. Stand together with other brave Knights

An axe works for me!

2. Strike repeatedly with a sharp or blunt object

3. Fire arrows at target

Hello, digi-bow!

4. Make use of traps

Hello, dirty tricks!

5. Use NEXO Powers

Prepare for an upload!

Always remember that you are not just defending the kingdom, you are representing its spirit and its future. Crush your opponents, but do it with honour and style.

HIDING
AND MASKING

Fighting monsters is harder than anyone
ever expects it to be. Monsters are
extremely powerful and their senses are very
sharp. A successful knight must be prepared
to attack these creatures using stealth and
camouflage.

Below are some helpful tips for beating
your monster opponent.

What about
snacks?
Can they smell
those too?

1. Brush your teeth. Monsters can smell your
last meal from a mile off.

Hey, that was only
that one time. And
maybe a few other
times too.

2. Avoid singing, whistling, or humming.
Seems obvious, but you'd be surprised at
how many knights hum their own theme
song whilst attacking.

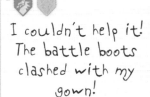

Or two . . .
Or more . . .

3. Practise moving silently and quickly so you can effectively sneak up on your opponent.

I couldn't help it! The battle boots clashed with my gown!

Ironie as always, Macy. Love it!

4. Avoid wearing high heels during surprise attacks.

Sorry, you'll have to talk to my personal publicity squirebot about that – he promotes and approves all my sneak attacks.

5. And don't bring personal publicity squirebots on secret missions.

TEAM MISSIONS –
WHAT'S IMPORTANT?

Finally, some advice about fighting as a NEXO KNIGHTS hero – a member of an elite team sworn to protect the kingdom of Knighton from all monster threats. They may not always agree, but they'll always be teammates!

CLAY: The Knight's Code and our experience as students at the Knights' Academy guide our every move on the battlefield. <u>There is no 'I' in 'team'.</u> But there is an 'e' in 'we'. And we will do our utmost to protect the kingdom and fight for justice and chivalry.

MACY: Wow, what can I say? I'd be nothing without those other fabulous NEXO KNIGHTS heroes around me. Even Lance. They make me the best mace-wielding princess that ever was. And even though sometimes we don't agree about strategy, I think we do all agree that we couldn't do what we do without everybody pitching in.

AXL: Hey, the guys have always got my back. I was from a little town in the Hill Country, and they all made me feel special and part of the group. Sure, I do the heavy lifting a lot of the time, but that's how I contribute to the team. Always remember: you do what you can and you try your best. That makes you a good teammate.

There is an I in Tiim: T.i.i.m. Man, can't you spell(?!)

AARON: Check it – I'm the knight who always pushes the team in gnarly new directions. Don't be afraid to think outside the box. Or, like, totally destroy the box and fly off on your shield! Look, I used to be all about pushing myself and doing crazy stunts all on my own. Not any more. Now it's about doing crazy things to help the team. What an off-the-shield thought is that, yo?

LANCE: The one thing that really makes this team function is . . . me. The rest of the NEXO KNIGHTS heroes fill a <u>supporting role</u>. They're adequate. Yes, that's the word . . .

LANCE: Fine, fine! If you want to know the real truth, I'm pretty lucky to have these other knights with me. Sure, they don't have great taste in haircare products, but they are, well, they're great. <u>They're always there for me.</u> OK, that felt good to say. Now, off to the Knight Club . . .

Lance! How would you like a Flying Macy on your backside!

Remember how we all started on that tournament team at the Knights' Academy?

Good times, big guy. Good times!

TEAMWORK

Clay Moorington here, with a few final thoughts on teamwork. Teamwork isn't just a thing . . . it's the ONLY thing. Without teamwork, the NEXO KNIGHTS heroes would be a disjointed, unruly, disorganized band of folk, tripping over themselves while holding pointy things. It would never work. But when we give up our own personal needs and desires to help the group succeed, well, we actually find that we always meet our own goals, too. Our team is amazing, strong and powerful. Though I think of myself as a true keeper of the Knight's Code, my fantastic teammates always show me new ways to live up to the code. Don't let them hear me say it, but I really love those guys!

Yo, Clay-man . . . I heard that! Love you too, bro!

Teamwork IS the most important thing.
(Other than lunch. And dinner. Oh, and breakfast.)

Let's face it, we wouldn't even be a team without Clay!

Clay is the only one I've met who comes close to living up to my high standards. Especially with a sword. That guy's always cleaving stuff.

WHAT THE CODE MEANS TO ME

All knights should be aware of what the Knight's Code means to them. Especially us NEXO KNIGHTS heroes, we must be ready to face the danger and defend our king and our people.

This is what it means to us . . .

THE CODE IS EVERYTHING TO ME. I'M NOT SURE HOW TO BE MORE SPECIFIC THAN THAT. IT RULES MY LIFE, MY THOUGHTS AND MY ACTIONS. AS THE CODE SAYS, 'I AM THE CODE. THE CODE IS ME'. WELL, IT DOESN'T ACTUALLY SAY THAT, BUT IT SHOULD – CLAY

Yes, like Clay says, the Knight's Code is important. But you know what's really important when you're a knight? Looking awesome. And that's something I do really well. Sure, you can be all noble and heroic, but no one will remember you unless you're rockin' some shiny armour and an even shinier smile. So don't just follow the Code, set the trend. Save the kingdom, but do it with style. That's the code according to Lance Richmond.

It's nowhere near as much fun sticking notes in this book when they actually ask you to do it. So I'll keep this short. The Code is cool. Enough said. Aaron out.

I believe in the Code. I believe in our kingdom. But I also believe we need to be more flexible. This is a complex world and 200 words written a few centuries ago may not have the answer to every single problem we're going to face in modern times. The Code is an excellent place to start, but I look at it more like this: the Code will guide us, but it does not have to command us - Macy

The Code makes sense to me. When I first got into the academy, I memorized the Code by writing its words in icing on my favourite cake. And then I ate the cake. It's kind of weird though, every time I think of the Code now, I get really hungry. Some people think the Code is everything. I think it's a deliciously sweet and frosted cake. But that's just me - Axl

THE END . . . ? OR JUST THE BEGINNING?

So, are we finished? :)

I'm guessing the monsters are 'Finished' now everyone's read this book. :P

THE MONSTERS ARE NOT FINISHED YET, SO REMEMBER WHAT YOU'VE LEARNED AND ALWAYS BE VIRTUOUS AND WORTHY, AND TRULY GREAT KNIGHTS.

Axl is the greatest one. :D

And you're still in pretty good shape, Clay! :)

ERM . . . SO AFTER READING THIS HANDBOOK YOU SHOULD NOW KNOW EVERYTHING . . .

I still don't know how to fit my hair under my helmet without messing it up. :)

Or how many cakes to eat before battle.

Or how many times Clay has read this book. :P

Or . . .

Sorry, guys, I need to stop your chat.
I think we have some company.

Preparing NEXO POWERS!

POWER OF UNIIIITED KNIIIIGHTS!

NEXOOOO KNIGHTS!